"Your arroga

"I wasn't aware I had point."

She just shook her head. Point to the prince.

"Have dinner with me tonight." Dima's expression left no doubt how he wanted the evening to end after their meal.

Or perhaps during. Honestly, the man looked hungry.

And Jenna liked it.

But she wasn't giving in that easily. Not to a man who was used to getting what he wanted, when he wanted it. Like all the Merikov princes.

They were wealthy, handsome and charismatic. A fatal combination for the hope of any level of humility.

"We haven't even eaten all of our lunch yet," she demurred.

"It's not food I'm thinking about."

Princesses by Royal Decree

Their place at the royal altar awaits...

The time has come for royal brothers King Nikolai and Princes Konstantin and Dimitri of Mirrus to wed. Their journeys to the altar will be just as they rule—by royal decree!

Lady Nataliya was contracted to marry a prince from Mirrus but is shocked when King Nikolai, whom she's secretly desired for years, steps in instead!

Emma's affair with Prince Konstantin is forced to end when his duty calls, but she's carrying a secret that will bind them forever!

Jenna's a fashion journalist and has no desire to be a princess, but her interest in Prince Dimitri could change everything...

Read Nataliya and Nikolai's story in
Queen by Royal Appointment

Read Emma and Konstantin's story in
His Majesty's Hidden Heir

And discover Jenna and Dimitri's story in
The Cost of Their Royal Fling

All available now!

Lucy Monroe

—

THE COST OF THEIR ROYAL FLING

Recycling programs for this product may not exist in your area.

ISBN-13: 978-1-335-56848-9

The Cost of Their Royal Fling

Copyright © 2022 by Lucy Monroe

All rights reserved. No part of this book may be used or reproduced in any manner whatsoever without written permission except in the case of brief quotations embodied in critical articles and reviews.

This is a work of fiction. Names, characters, places and incidents are either the product of the author's imagination or are used fictitiously. Any resemblance to actual persons, living or dead, businesses, companies, events or locales is entirely coincidental.

This edition published by arrangement with Harlequin Books S.A.

For questions and comments about the quality of this book, please contact us at CustomerService@Harlequin.com.

Harlequin Enterprises ULC
22 Adelaide St. West, 41st Floor
Toronto, Ontario M5H 4E3, Canada
www.Harlequin.com

Printed in U.S.A.

USA TODAY bestselling author **Lucy Monroe** lives and writes in the gorgeous Pacific Northwest. While she loves her home, she delights in experiencing different cultures and places on her travels, which she happily shares with her readers through her books. A lifelong devotee of the romance genre, Lucy can't imagine a more fulfilling career than writing the stories in her head for her readers to enjoy.

Books by Lucy Monroe

Harlequin Presents

Kostas's Convenient Bride
The Spaniard's Pleasurable Vengeance
After the Billionaire's Wedding Vows...

Ruthless Russians

An Heiress for His Empire
A Virgin for His Prize

Princesses by Royal Decree

Queen by Royal Appointment
His Majesty's Hidden Heir

Visit the Author Profile page
at Harlequin.com for more titles.

For my amazing husband, who has always been my strongest advocate and most enthusiastic support. You've given me over three decades of love and laughter, honey, and I'm looking foward to many more.

CHAPTER ONE

Frank Sinatra singing "My Way" startled Prince Dimitri from his perusal of the United Mining contract.

It was the most important deal of his career to date. Dimitri wasn't going to allow a single poorly worded sentence to remain in the entire thirty-two-page document.

He tapped the screen on his phone, accepting the video call before the crooner started singing again. "Isn't this a little early for you?" he asked by way of greeting to his middle brother.

Konstantin and his wife made their home in Seattle, a time zone three hours behind his in New York.

His brother made a scoffing sound, his expression disbelieving. "It's only seven thirty a.m. over there, but there you are, in your office, chained to your desk already."

Dimitri shrugged. "So? I would have thought *you* would still be in bed with your lovely wife."

He had no wife and children to keep him in his sleek penthouse apartment through breakfast, much less in bed once he'd woken. Dimitri had been in his office since six a.m. and would no doubt still be here at six p.m. His executive assistant and their team would show up at eight a.m. These hours on his own, without interruptions, were usually some of his most productive.

"You need a life outside work," his brother chided.

Dimitri leaned back in his chair, working the kinks out of his neck. "Being older doesn't give you license to play agony aunt."

Even on the small phone screen, his brother's offence showed clearly in his expression. "I am no one's agony aunt, but I am your big brother, and you should listen to me. Wisdom comes with age, you know."

"You're a whole eight years older. Hardly a generation," Dimitri scoffed.

"Dima, I'm serious." Kon was no longer smiling but looking concerned. "You need a life outside your job."

"I go to the gym six days a week." He broke his day up with exercise and strength training midmorning. "I have my triathlons."

He was highly competitive, but all that training had to have a purpose, and Dimitri competed in triathlons throughout the year.

"If you were on a team, that might mean something, but you're an independent competitor."

"It is still something besides work."

"You were such a friendly child, but you've grown up to be such an isolationist."

"We all grow up eventually." Dimitri had reveled in his role as youngest son and prince, making friends easily and being a hell of a lot more social than he was now, until he'd entered the military.

Unlike his older brothers who had served in roles that would not put them in active danger, as the youngest son, Dimitri had been allowed to see combat. That time had changed him. Losing his best friend and other comrades to the violence of war had changed him. Losing the woman he thought he would marry had changed him.

The lesson he'd started learning at the age of six when

he lost his mother to cancer had solidified in his twenties. Life was about loss.

The more people you let into your life, the more people you lost.

It was that simple. The profit and loss statement was heavily balanced in one direction.

He let no one else in. His potential for emotional pain was minimized.

"How are the boys?" Dimitri asked, when his brother didn't immediately get to the point of his early morning phone call.

His nephew, Valentin, was six and half years younger than brother Mikhail, who was now nine. Having learned from one of the best, Konstantin's son was just as good an older brother as his father had always been to Dimitri.

Dimitri had lucked out with both of his older siblings, not that he would ever admit that to either of them.

"Mishka is frighteningly mature for his age, and Valentin is never happier than when he is exploring." Pride rang loud and clear in Konstantin's voice. "They both miss their uncle."

"I will schedule a trip to Seattle soon."

"That is the hope."

"I hardly think making sure I come to visit my nephews soon was worth you leaving Emma and a warm bed for this phone call."

The expression on Kon's face said he agreed. So what was going on?

Dimitri waited in silence to find out.

Kon frowned and rubbed his face. "Growing up does not mean cutting yourself off from the joy of relationships, friendship or otherwise."

Dimitri's inner radar blipped. "You've been talking to Dad."

"He just wants to see you happy."

Their father had too much time on his hands since his health had forced him to abdicate the throne to Nikolai.

"I am happy as I am."

"Are you?" Only family could put so much meaning into two simple words.

However, Dimitri refused to be drawn into that discussion. Moments of loneliness were to be expected and not something he would ever discuss with his father or brothers. Though royalty, they were a close family. That *did not* mean he wanted to have some emotion-laden conversation with his older brother.

Sarcasm and business were their language currency, and he was pleased to keep it that way. "I am."

"You could be happier."

Seriously? Dimitri gave his brother a disbelieving stare. "Says you."

"But this is not actually why I dragged myself from my wife's bed so freaking early and snuck off to make a phone call."

Could have fooled him.

"Snuck off? That sounds serious." Even more serious was the fact his brother had been putting off the real reason for his call.

Whatever it was, it wasn't something Kon wanted to talk about, and that put Dimitri's instincts on alert.

Nevertheless, he joked, "I don't see Emma monitoring your calls."

"No, but I don't want her to hear this." Kon grimaced. "She's practically as close to Jenna as Nataliya is at this point. They're like three sisters by different mothers."

"And?" What did the sexy best friend to his sister-in-law, the Queen of Mirrus, have to do with anything?

"Nataliya is all right?" His brain automatically went there.

His sister-in-law had had a life-risking miscarriage a month after Dimitri's return from deployment.

He hadn't even known she was pregnant. Still in their first trimester, Nataliya and Nikolai had shared the news with no one.

Except perhaps Jenna, the fashion journalist that was like a sister to Nataliya, and now apparently Kon's wife, Emma. Dimitri hadn't noticed the three women growing that close, but then, with his office on the other side of the continent from his brothers' as well as their island country of Mirrus, he did not spend as much time with his family as his father would have liked.

Work kept Dimitri busy, though. He was determined to ensure the future stability of the company Mirrus Global, and by extension the country to which he had been born prince. It was his honor and his duty.

"She's pregnant again," Konstantin answered, his expression anything but pleased.

"Surely that is good news."

Konstantin nodded. "Of course it is, but after the last time, it is imperative she be exposed to nothing stressful."

While Dimitri agreed, he did not know how realistic a goal that was for the Queen of Mirrus. "And there is something you think I can do to minimize her stress?"

"Yes."

"I cannot imagine what," Dimitri answered honestly. "Though naturally, I will do whatever I can."

"I expected no less."

Nor should Kon have. All three brothers had been raised with a strong sense of duty. Dimitri's time in combat had only intensified his own sense of responsibility. Being the officer in charge when lives were lost had taught him how high the cost could be of making even the smallest error in judgment.

"Someone close to the family is leaking sensitive information to the press." Kon said it baldly, with no buildup.

Dimitri sat up straighter, barely holding himself back from leaping to his feet. He was careful not to reveal too much of his inner thoughts or feelings. The practice was so ingrained, it came as second nature to him, even with his family.

"Personal or business?" he asked Konstantin in an even tone.

He didn't ask if his brother was sure, or how he'd come to that conclusion. It was enough that he had.

"Both."

Dimitri very deliberately bit out an expletive.

"Exactly."

"You do not know who it is?"

He framed it as a question, but Dimitri had no doubt he was right. If Konstantin knew the name of the culprit, he would have named him.

"Not as such, no."

"What does that mean?"

"The leaks happen after Jenna has been to visit Nataliya."

Something inside Dimitri seized painfully. Jenna had been accepted into the inner circle of their family by all of them. If she had betrayed them, it would devastate more than Nataliya.

His father looked on the beautiful fashion journalist as a daughter, just as he did his daughter-in-law, Nataliya.

From the moment Nataliya and Nikolai became engaged, Jenna had been a frequent visitor to the palace. She and his father shared a love for reality television that frankly had the rest of the family baffled. Dimitri had thought Jenna was humoring the former king at first, but had soon realized she was as interested in the lives of celebrity strangers as his father.

"Impossible," Dimitri said after a second's thought. "Jenna would never betray the sister of her heart."

Jenna had shown her loyalty to Nataliya time and again. She'd been vocal about how much she valued her place among the royal family, if equally outspoken about how much she had no desire to actually be one of them.

The woman with strongly feminist ideals had no desire to be a princess.

Konstantin sighed, suddenly looking like a man who had gotten up two hours early to make a secret phone call. "I would have thought not, but the timing cannot be denied. It has happened too many times to be coincidence."

"Either she's leaking information," Dimitri mused, still not convinced, "or someone she trusts enough to talk about us is doing it."

The latter seemed far more likely.

"That was my thought."

"Have you asked her?"

"Are you kidding me? What do you think is the first thing she would do after such a conversation?"

"Call Nataliya." And that would cause stress for the queen. "You really think Jenna would upset Nataliya right now?"

"Perhaps not on purpose, but even if she just lets it slip we suspected her, you don't think that will upset our sister-in-law?"

"Sure, but I'm not convinced someone as intelligent and caring as Jenna would let something like that slip to Nataliya when the queen's health could be at risk from stress."

"If not Nataliya, then my wife."

And that would lead to major stress for Konstantin. Dimitri got it.

"I still do not think there is any way Jenna would leak privileged information to the media," Dimitri informed his brother. "Or even talk about us to someone she trusts. She's too savvy for that. She's a journalist, after all."

"The timing, Dima."

Enough occurrences that it could not be a coincidence. That was concerning. As was the timing of the leak.

"I'm in the middle of an important but potentially fragile negotiation bringing several small countries together in a joint business venture," Dimitri informed his brother.

"Why have I heard nothing about it?"

"Because I'm still going over the information packet before sending it on to you and Nikolai."

Konstantin nodded. "There are a lot of reasons why another leak could be damaging, but I'll number that among them."

"Agreed. What exactly is it you want from me?" Dimitri asked.

"Find out if Jenna is the leak, and if she's not, who is."

"That sounds like a job for a security consultant."

"Nikolai wants everything kept between us. If Jenna is the cause of the leak, he doesn't want there to be even a chance that information could be made public."

His brother, the king, wanted to protect his wife's feelings, whatever the circumstance. Dimitri admired Nikolai's concern for his wife but was glad he had no such relationship to navigate.

He preferred the freedom to pursue his interests with unfettered ruthlessness.

"You live in Seattle. Why am I being tasked with this?"

"I've done my best to discern the truth and cannot do so without making myself suspicious to my wife."

"You don't think Jenna would be suspicious if I just showed up on her doorstep asking questions?"

"I trust you are capable of a great deal more subtlety than that."

"You want me to date her?" He wasn't some undercover spy.

"Would that really be a hardship?"

Dimitri hid his knee-jerk reaction. Going to bed with the beautiful woman would be no hardship at all. Dating her? That implied the kind of relationship he did not do.

And it smacked of dishonesty.

So maybe his honor had some fetters on his ruthlessness, but that wasn't something he needed to share with his older brother.

Konstantin sighed. "Look, Dima, I don't care if you date her or invite her to participate in one of your triathlons. Just figure out a way to get close enough to determine where the leak is coming from."

"She's not a triathlete."

"She runs. She swims. Teach her how to ride a bike competitively."

Dimitri just shook his head at his brother's ignorance.

"I'll be in Seattle at the end of the week." But he was handling this thing as he saw fit.

Jenna Beals put down her phone, equal parts excited and worried for her best friend.

Nataliya, Queen of Mirrus, was pregnant again. After her last pregnancy had ended in a miscarriage and her nearly hemorrhaging to death, Jenna had assumed the other woman wouldn't try to get pregnant again.

Silly her.

Although Nataliya had given birth to both the heir, six-year-old daughter Anna Yelena, and the spare, three-year-old Daniil, it turned out the queen adored being a mother and wanted more children.

Children. As in plural.

Since Nataliya's miscarriage and subsequent bleeding had been diagnosed as idiopathic, which meant they didn't *know* what caused it, there was as much chance it could happen again as not.

So Jenna worried, but she couldn't help being happy for her friend too. Because Nataliya? Was over the moon.

Jenna would have to plan a trip to Mirrus soon, just to confirm to herself that her friend was doing as well as she claimed.

Her heart sped just a little with the usual fillip of excitement at the thought of seeing another certain member of the royal family. Prince Dimitri: Dima.

The youngest and, in her opinion, sexiest of the three Merikov brothers, the six-and-a-half-foot-tall triathlete had a gorgeous body. With brown hair and gorgeous gray eyes, he was her own personal brand of catnip, but the prince was five years younger than Jenna. He was also the brother-in-law of her best friend. Then there was that pesky *prince* thing.

He was off limits to Jenna's libido on so many levels, it would take a skyscraper elevator to reach him.

A trip she was in no way willing to take.

Forcing her thoughts away from the delectable man, Jenna went back to work on the spread for the sustainable fashion article her magazine was featuring that month. The plus-size model, who had opened her own wardrobe for the photo shoot, had a ginormous following that had only grown after she'd caught the notice of a pop icon.

The interview and photo spread had the potential to be one of their most popular to date, and that included the dating and wedding spreads she'd done on Nataliya.

"Hey, Jenna, there's someone here to see you."

Jenna looked up, about to ask who it was, only to look into the gray eyes she saw way too often in her dreams.

Dreams that left her feeling hot and breathless.

"Dima!" she exclaimed in shock. "What are you doing here?"

It was as if her thoughts of him had conjured up the one guy she could not let herself go for.

Casually, for him, dressed in a spring-weight designer suit sans tie, he stood in a relaxed pose opposite her desk. "Kon asked me to come visit the boys."

His security detail must be outside the door, only knowing Dima, he could as easily left them in the lobby, or downstairs. He took more liberties with them than his brothers.

There were benefits to being third in line, she supposed.

"I meant here in my office, not Seattle." Though Dima didn't visit the West Coast as often as his family would have liked, the fact he was in the city wasn't that surprising.

That he was standing in front of her desk startled her usual cool right out of Jenna.

"I had some time on my hands."

"So you came here?" Why?

He gave her the charming smile that was featured so often in the papers when his picture was taken. Only she'd noticed how it no longer reached his eyes since his deployment. No one else in his royal family seemed to find Dima much changed.

Nataliya did, though.

She wanted to ask him about it, but knew doing so would draw them closer together, something she could not afford with her ridiculous sexual fixation on the man.

"So you came here? When you are in town to see the children?" His sister-in-law, Emma, would be delighted.

Dima was a favorite with his nephews, and Emma liked anything that made her sons happy.

"They are in school, and Emma and Kon are both working, so here I am."

He made it sound like the most natural thing in the world, but it couldn't be much further from that.

"Why aren't you?" she asked. "Working, I mean."

His smile this time reached his gaze, but those gray eyes were filled with humor. At her expense. "Perhaps you have not noticed, but it is lunchtime."

She flicked a gaze to her computer monitor. Sure enough, it was twelve thirty. "Maybe I don't take lunch until one."

"More like you don't take lunch at all and sit at your desk with one of those disgusting protein bars." The words reminded Jenna that they still had an audience.

Skylar, the editorial assistant who had led Dima to her office without giving Jenna a heads-up that a prince was here to see her. The woman would have made a lousy receptionist. It was a good thing she was more interested in the journalism side of working for the magazine.

Speaking of... "Where's Rose?"

The receptionist guarded her desk and the inner sanctum behind it with the tenacity of a trained secret service agent.

"She's at lunch," Jenna's assistant offered helpfully.

"As you should be." Oh, Dima might be the youngest, but he had the princely arrogance down pat.

"And you are here to make sure I eat?" she asked mockingly, not believing it for a minute.

"It sounds like someone needs to." He gave Skylar a conspiratorial look. "Protein bars? Really?"

"Some of us actually live our lives without a personal chef." Did that sound snide?

Maybe a little, but sarcasm came as naturally to Jenna as breathing. Dima had never been offended before by it.

If the wry tilt of his lips was any indication, he wasn't offended now either. "How long do you need to button things up?"

"You're assuming I'm coming to lunch with you."

"Not immediately." He sounded like he expected accolades for the accommodation.

"You are a piece of work, Your Highness."

"I prefer Dima."

"Since when?" She used the honorific as a barrier between them.

A reminder of their age gap and his familial relationship to Nataliya.

And because she'd always assumed it annoyed him. He'd corrected his brothers and Nataliya often enough over the years.

Not that his family took any notice. To them, Prince Dimitri was, and always would be, Dima.

"Since hearing it in that snarky tone you use. It sounds more like a pet name coming from you than a reminder of my role as youngest in my family." His honesty took her breath away.

It also let her know that she had achieved the opposite of her intent.

"Are you two like a thing?" Skylar asked, her interest practically vibrating off her.

The look Dima gave the woman could have frozen concrete. "Do you work for a fashion magazine, or for a gossip rag?"

The younger woman gave Dima a flirtatious smile. "Sometimes they're the same thing."

"Not this magazine," Jenna informed her. "We don't

peddle gossip, and you should know better than to speculate about something like that, especially out loud."

Giving up any hope of getting more work done until
after she'd had lunch with Dima, Jenna shut down her system and stood up. "For your information, His Highness and
I are not dating. We are not sleeping together, and if I hear
anything to the contrary, I'll know exactly who to yell at."

Not that Jenna was known for yelling, but hopefully
Skylar would take note that in this case, she would be
more than willing to.

The younger woman gave Jenna a disbelieving look. So,
not intimidated. "I don't think I'm the only one who hasn't
left for lunch who's wondering the same thing."

"You've got no sense of self-preservation, do you?"
Dima asked, his own tone disbelieving.

"What? Jenna isn't the type of boss to bury me under
bad assignments because I irritated her. She's not like that."

Jenna didn't mind the confirmation that she had a reputation for being fair-minded and practical. However, she
didn't like knowing her editorial assistant thought that
sense of fair play meant Jenna wouldn't come down on
her like a ton of bricks. Because she so would.

"Good to know," Dima said calmly. "However, I am a
man who takes my privacy very seriously, and I am not
nearly so forgiving."

Jenna knew she could trust Dima with her life, and
still she wouldn't have liked being on the receiving end
of that look.

This was the ruthless prince that few had met, but those
who knew him even remotely well would assume lived
under his urbane exterior.

No way could Dima have done some of the deals he had
since taking over the New York office for Mirrus Global
if he didn't have a deep and well-utilized ruthless streak.

"It's not like I was going to spread any rumors," Skylar assured them hastily, her expression not nearly so sanguine. "I was curious, that's all."

Dima didn't look like he bought it. Jenna wasn't sure she did either. This particular young editor was known for how much she liked to gossip.

Showing a recently wakened sense of self-preservation, though, Skylar gulped, gave a weak smile, and took herself off.

Jenna grabbed her purse and cardigan. "I think you intimidated her."

"I am a prince. She should have been intimidated from the moment of meeting me."

"I can't tell if you are serious or not."

"Why wouldn't I be serious?" He sounded genuinely curious. "Most people are awed to some degree by royalty."

"I guess that's reason one hundred and fifty-nine that I'm glad my BFF is the queen and not me."

What looked like satisfaction flashed in his gray gaze. "You are unique, Jenna. You have never been awed by my family. I remember when you called my brother King Yummy."

Jenna laughed. She still called him that sometimes, to tease Nataliya. To tease a king who seemed to take life more seriously the older he got.

CHAPTER TWO

THEY WALKED INTO a Michelin-starred Asian fusion restaurant on the waterfront. "Oh, I've heard amazing things about this place," Jenna said with approval.

Those royal pearly whites flashed. "Glad to know I pleased, but I'm surprised you have not been here before."

Jenna just smiled and shook her head. When lunch would probably cost more than her car payment, this was not someplace that could make it onto her restaurants to try list.

Not to mention the weeks-long wait on reservations, which begged the question: How had he gotten them in for an impromptu lunch?

Or had lunch not been impromptu at all?

Whoever had done the decor was a minimalist with a preference for Japanese artwork, green plants and teak wood. A water feature trickled down the center of one wall over flat natural stones.

Jenna's stress level went down several notches as they stepped into the peaceful dining area. The noise level was low despite every table being filled. The architect and interior designers had done their job and then some.

"You had to have made reservations," she remarked.

And still, he'd offered to wait while she finished what she was working on.

"The chef is an old friend," Dima said dismissively. Like that was no big deal. "He keeps this table for his guests."

The table they'd been led to was nearer the kitchens, but not even remotely poorly located. Though she had to admit that none of the tables were situated in a spot she would have considered less than ideal.

"You have *old* friends?" she teased. "You're barely thirty."

"Is that like being barely pregnant?" he asked sardonically. "Either you are, or you aren't. I am in fact thirty. You were there for the ridiculous cake Nataliya insisted on."

Nataliya had done an Over the Hill party for Dima's thirtieth as a joke, since thirty was in no way over the hill and the man was the youngest adult in the family.

"The cake was supposed to be shaped like a hill."

"It looked like a pile of manure with green bits. Not at all appetizing."

The epic fail had been funnier than the party theme. "It tasted good, though."

He pulled her chair out for her, subtly maneuvering the maître d' out of the way. "It didn't taste like it looked, and for that I should probably be grateful."

"She was trying to give a new baker a chance." Jenna smiled up at Dima as she settled into her seat.

The maître d' placed her napkin over her lap, and Jenna murmured, "Thank you."

The woman moved away quietly after Dima had taken his seat. The table could seat four but was still intimate for two.

"Well, I don't see the bakery getting a lot of orders off of that monstrosity of a cake," Dima opined.

"Then you're very short-sighted," Jenna informed him. "Nataliya told me the baker has been inundated with orders for novelty cakes since pictures of your party went viral."

"To each their own."

She laughed. "You can be such a snob."

"Because I don't want to eat food that looks like it's already digested?"

"Don't be gross. I'd like to eat my lunch now without that image in my head, thank you."

"I beg your pardon. I did not mean to put you off your feed."

Jenna burst into laughter. "I'm not a horse."

"No, you are not." The look he gave her was all male appreciation.

"Don't look at me like that. You are practically my own brother." Oh, that was such a lie.

"Again, either you are, or you are not," he informed her wryly. "You and I share no blood relation, or any legal relation either, for that matter."

"You are my best friend's little brother-in-law." That felt less like the deterrent she'd always told herself it was.

He gave her another heated, purely adult look. "Hardly little."

"Oh, brother, you are laying it on thick." And it was working. Jenna's body was zinging with *want* and *now* and *give me some*. "The question is: Why?"

He shrugged. "Why look at you like you are a beautiful woman? Because you are. Why look at you like I want you? Because I do."

"What?" She looked around furtively, but no one was paying them any attention. "You can't just blurt stuff like that out."

"Why not?"

"Because."

"You're strangely lacking in words for a journalist."

"I shouldn't have to tell you. Wasn't Skylar's reaction earlier enough? Regardless of what either of us said, the rumors we are dating are going to be all over our offices by the time I go home tonight."

"So?"

"So? We aren't dating!"

"We could be."

"What are you saying? You want to date me?"

"Don't look so horrified. I didn't say I wanted to court you; I'm fully aware of your aversion to being a princess. We can date…" He paused, letting their eyes meet and hold while the sexual tension between them built. "And other things, if we want. You are single. I have no commitments of that nature. Neither of us is looking for marriage or expecting long-term commitment of any kind."

"We aren't?" she asked, thinking he took a lot for granted. "Why? Because I'm not some kind of nobility?"

He didn't even bother to look worried, just patient. "Because you've made it clear over and over again how little desire you have to be an actual part of a royal family," he spelled out. "No matter how close you are to mine."

"That's true." And he'd been listening.

The waiter approached their table and placed a starter in front of them both.

"I hope you do not mind, but I when I am here, the chef selects my food."

"I like the adventure of that, but it surprises me you cede the control," she replied with candor.

The barely there tilt of his lips couldn't quite be called a smile, but the expression reached his eyes, so Jenna took it as a win.

"Control is an illusion in most things."

"You did not just say that." Such a sentiment was not the type expressed by the men in his family.

The women either, for that matter.

"You learn a lot about what you do and do not control

when lives are in the balance." He shrugged. "Besides, who better to select my food than the man who prepared it?"

"You said he was an old friend. You must trust him a lot."

"I've had to trust him with my life."

"He was in the military with you?"

"He was in an American unit that worked closely with our Mirrusian one."

"So, not such an *old* friend."

"My last combat tour was six years ago."

"That's not even a whole decade," she chided with humor.

"You can die in an instant and live a lifetime in a year."

Jenna couldn't argue that bit of wisdom.

"I have no desire to get married anytime soon either," Dima said, picking up the thread of their conversation before the waiter's arrival with their starter, like they hadn't had a whole other chat between times. "No matter what plans my father might have."

"You're saying Prince Evengi would never convince you to sign a contract like he got Konstantin to do."

"No."

"You're so sure." Jenna wasn't as certain as he was. "You are every bit as duty-driven as either of your brothers."

"And I will do my duty," he readily agreed. "On my own timetable."

Laughter burst out of her. "I did not think it was possible, but you are possibly even more stubborn and arrogant than your older brothers."

"The privilege of being the youngest." His tone was as good as a shrug.

"You don't deny being arrogant?"

"I would term it *confident*, but I do not see arrogance as an undesirable trait."

"You wouldn't."

"It takes confidence to achieve one's goals."

"Sometimes it takes patience."

"I have plenty of that when I need it as well."

She made a scoffing sound.

"If you doubt me, ask any of the men I served with. War requires a lot of waiting."

"Does it?" Jenna knew very little about life in the military.

"Yes. Especially on the types of missions my elite team was sent on."

"It always surprised me that you were actually in combat. Neither of your brothers was allowed."

"As the youngest, it was my duty."

The very concept horrified her, but Jenna did her best to keep her expression neutral. Royal families did things differently. "I don't understand. Why was that your duty?"

"Neither of my brothers could be risked by serving in a war zone, but not to have a member of our family serve in an active unit when we asked other members our military to do so would be cowardly."

"What if there had only been two brothers?"

"Then Konstantin would have waited to do his military service until after Nikolai had fathered his first child."

"Konstantin would have gone into combat, though?"

"Yes."

"Being royal has a lot of unseen expectations."

"Especially for a ruling royal family."

"You do realize that it is medieval to have ruling authority based solely on the circumstances of your birth."

He gave her a look that couldn't be termed anything but

indulgent. "It is also twenty-first century. We are hardly the only royal ruling family in the world."

Okay, so he had a point. "Even so, I don't understand why your brother, who seems to be a very progressive thinker, hasn't instituted a constitutional monarchy."

"You might be surprised to know that my father considered doing so."

"Wow." That was surprising.

With uncanny prescience, Dima stopped talking again, and seconds later, the waiter approached to clear away their starter. Another of the waitstaff placed their lunches before them before stepping away without a word.

Dima took a bite of the soba noodles mixed with vegetables and chewed appreciatively. "That is good," he said after swallowing.

Jenna agreed, having tried it herself and loving the umami seasoning with a hint of lemongrass. "It's a mix of Vietnamese and Japanese flavors."

They ate in silence for a moment or two before Jenna asked about the surprising revelation Dima had made.

"It was before my birth. I had no part in the decision."

Though clearly it was something that had been talked about years later, or Dima wouldn't know about it. "But His Highness told you about it."

"Do you realize that my father is the only person in my family you consistently use formal address with?"

She shrugged. "I think he prefers it."

"Perhaps." Dima took a sip of his seltzer water. "In answer to your question, yes, Father told my brothers and me about it."

"Why didn't he do follow through? He wouldn't have considered it if he didn't think it was a good idea."

"You are right, but ultimately, Father and his advisors

determined that the potential for instability to Mirrus was too great."

"Of course, they did." Her cynicism leaked into her voice, but Jenna had seen too many men, and women too, if she was being honest, refuse to let go of the power they had grown accustomed to wielding.

"You sound dismissive. I assure you, both he and, later, my brother examined the issue very closely."

"But holding on to power was easier."

"Holding on to power, as you term it, nearly cost my father his life. It was the main reason my eldest brother's first marriage was an unhappy one. The personal cost of maintaining the ruling monarchy has been great to my family, but ultimately the good of Mirrus must come first."

"The good as you define it."

"Yes."

She respected that he didn't try to dress up his agreement. One of the things she liked about Dima was that he didn't apologize for his beliefs.

He was a good man, but yes, a very arrogant one as well.

"I could never be part of making choices for other people without their say-so."

"Mirrus is no dictatorship. My brother holds court, listening to our citizens and their concerns for one entire day each week. Furthermore, unlike a dictatorship, our citizens have the ability to emigrate whenever they wish, and because of our diplomatic ties with other countries, options for many to settle in."

"That's still not the same as a democracy."

"Where oligarchs make most of the power decisions behind the scenes with money and deals that will never see the light of day?" Dima asked with heavy mockery.

"It's not always like that."

"Your optimism is charming."

"Your arrogance is showing again."

"I wasn't aware I had tucked it away at some point."

She just shook her head. Point to the prince.

"Have dinner with me tonight." Dima's expression left no doubt how he wanted the evening to end after their meal.

Or perhaps during. Honestly, the man looked hungry.

And Jenna liked it.

But she wasn't giving in that easily. Not to a man who was used to getting what he wanted, when he wanted it. Like all the Merikov princes.

They were wealthy, handsome and charismatic. A fatal combination for the hope of any level of humility.

"We haven't even eaten all of our lunch yet," she demurred.

"It's not food I'm thinking about."

"I'm not hopping into your bed, Dima." No matter how much her body might be urging her to do that very thing.

"But you want to."

"Are you always this blunt?"

"No."

"Why me?"

"Why do I want you?"

"No." She didn't think she'd survive a listing of what he found sexually appealing about her over lunch. "Why so blunt with me?"

"You appreciate honesty."

"I do." And once again, he'd noticed. He listened.

She liked it.

His dark brow lifted in sexy inquiry. "So?"

"So, you are honest to the point of bluntness."

"Would you rather I was more subtle?" he asked like he really wanted an answer.

Jenna realized that no, she didn't want that. "I prefer the bluntness."

It should be easier to combat. Just say *no*. Only she was struggling with that one small word.

"You're five years younger than me," she said instead.

His gray gaze pierced hers. "If I were a teenager, that might matter. At the age of thirty, it does not signify."

"To you."

"Does it bother you?" This time his question came out as more of a challenge.

It had. When they'd first met, and she was lusting after a twenty-two-year-old who hadn't ever had a serious girlfriend, as far as Jenna knew. And because he was a prince with a significant public profile, she thought she would have known.

When he'd started dating Galena, it had certainly gone public.

"Jenna?" he prompted. "Are you really bothered by such an insignificant thing?"

"No." At least not in the terms he'd outlined. Dating. Sex. Casual. "But if it did bother me, it would not be insignificant."

"Point taken." His smile was sexy and natural.

It was also really devastating to the one part of her she didn't want affected by this man.

Her heart.

The truth was, Jenna was enjoying lunch with Dima a lot more than was good for her. She'd always found the youngest Merikov brother likable, if arrogant, but in dating mode?

He was a force of nature, his animal magnetism drawing her.

Charming and urbane, he willingly discussed topics of

interest to her, showing a wide breadth of knowledge on subjects she found surprising.

"You're well-read on sustainable fashion."

"The fast fashion industry feeds too many societal ills for me to ignore its impact. It is important that my brothers and I are aware of the societal and environmental impact of any company we choose to do business with."

"Not all CEOs feel the same."

As CEO, Dima's oldest brother, King Nikolai, was the nominal head of Mirrus Global, the family-owned international conglomeration. Konstantin was the chief operating officer, and Dima was the chief financial officer, but the truth was, all three brothers shared certain responsibilities while delineating others.

That delineation could be geographical, like Nikolai running the offices on Mirrus, Konstantin controlling those in Seattle, and Dima heading the New York office. Jenna knew the brothers also had certain assigned work responsibilities they trusted each other, while still working closely together.

"Is it hard for you to live so far from your family?" His other brothers were a couple of hours' flight from each other.

Even with a private jet at his disposal, Dima had to travel a good portion of the day to reach his closest family in Seattle, though.

"No."

"But you're such a close knit family."

His gorgeous mouth twisted in a slight grimace. "Since my time in the military, I have preferred a certain amount of privacy that distance makes more possible."

"You are still in the military, aren't you?"

Something serious flashed in his gray eyes. "I should have said active deployment. Yes, I have followed tradition and retain an officer position in our country's military. When my father finally retires as brigadier general, it is expected I will be in a position to succeed him."

"Not Nikolai?" she asked.

"It has traditionally been the role of a younger son, but my father was an only child."

"Oh." Her dearest friend had been married to the King of Mirrus for the better part of a decade, and there was still so much about the royal family that Jenna did not know.

The alarm on her phone sounded. Regret at what it meant swept over Jenna as she swiped the screen before the chimes could annoy the other diners. "I have an afternoon editorial meeting. I have to go."

Dima stood immediately, grabbing his own phone and sending a text. "I'll drop you off."

"But what about paying?"

"Sorted before we arrived."

"It must be nice."

"Many aspects of my life are *nice*. Just as many are challenging."

She thought that wasn't something he admitted readily to others, so Jenna took the confidence for the honor that it was.

Dima drove her the few blocks back to her office but stayed her with a hand on her arm before she exited the car. "What time would you like me to pick you up?"

"For dinner?" she asked. Had she agreed to that?

His gray eyes sent messages likely to make breathing difficult. "To start."

"You are persistent."

"It goes with the stubborn arrogance." Charm. He had it.

And Prince Dimitri of Mirrus was fully aware of just how charming he was.

She gave him a wry look. "I'll say."

His smile sent tingles of arousal to places she couldn't focus on minutes before going into a conference room filled with her colleagues.

"Don't Emma and Konstantin expect you for dinner?" He was in town to visit his nephews, after all.

"Yes."

"Well then."

"Join us." His finger brushed over the pulse on her wrist. "Emma will be disappointed if you don't."

"I'm being maneuvered, I think."

He shrugged, clearly unrepentant.

"You'll tell her you invited me, won't you?"

"Naturally."

Jenna shook her head, but she was smiling.

"Is that a *no*?"

"That's a *you're too much* head shake, but I'll be there. Emma would be hurt if she found out you had invited me and I said no." If Jenna had had other plans, that would have been fine.

But she didn't, and Jenna made it a practice never to lie to her friends, not even to get out of doing things she didn't want to do. In this case, she wanted to have dinner with the charming man a little too much.

She tried not to lie at all, but sometimes finessing the truth saved a lot of hurt feelings. Especially in the fashion industry.

CHAPTER THREE

Jenna changed her outfit for the third time and said a word she didn't usually say. This should be no big deal. How many times had she shared a meal with Kon and Emma and their two adorable sons? Too many to count.

She had even done so when Dima was there as well. The only difference tonight was that she was arriving with him.

After spending lunch flirting.

He'd made his sexual interest in her known.

Blatantly.

It had been a lot easier to think of him as King Nikolai's kid brother when Jenna had thought the desire was one-sided. Not that she hadn't noticed him looking at her over the years, but she'd convinced herself she'd been mistaken about the heat she'd seen in his gaze.

Why would he be interested in a woman five years his senior and not the supermodel type that usually vied for his attention?

At five-foot-six, with an average figure and a little above average bra size, Jenna would never be described as tall and willowy. Elegant.

She could dress that way, of course, but her default was more relaxed fashion, not to mention sustainable. Jenna wouldn't be gracing the covers of any glossy magazines, but that didn't mean she wanted Dima to look at her and see nothing but average.

Not usually so lacking in confidence, Jenna glared ruefully at the pile of discarded clothes on her bed.

All of this for Dima? Her best friend's kid brother? Or as good as.

He was no less off-limits in terms of a relationship than ever, but then, Dima wasn't offering her a relationship.

He was offering sex.

And if her instincts were on target, he was offering really good, really satisfying sex.

The kind of sex she hadn't had in too long.

Maybe since meeting the youngest prince.

Not that Jenna had been celibate, but physical intimacy was never as satisfying as she expected it to be anymore.

She'd dated guys who were tall like Dima. Well-built like Dima. Even men with the same espresso-brown hair and gray eyes like Dima. Men who were older than Dima, more experienced.

Or so she convinced herself.

And not one of them had made it past a few dates and maybe a night or two in her bed.

None had held her interest. None invaded her dreams. None made her ache with wanting in the middle of the night when no one was there to see.

Not like Dima.

And today Dima had made it clear he was looking back. He wanted her.

He wasn't looking for long-term, and she was glad. Even if Jenna could stomach the idea of being royalty, she could never be the wife Dima needed her to be.

She would always be five years older than him.

Sterile, she would not be able to give him children, heirs the throne required.

Even as third son to the former king, Dima was expected to have children. His father, Prince Evengi, talked about it enough.

Dima had a responsibility to both the throne and to his family in that regard. Her sterility was something she simply could not and would not change.

So his lack of desire for anything serious was in her favor.

If a tiny part of her heart that Jenna had shut off long ago grieved that truth, she ignored it. Like she'd been doing for most of her adult life.

What she could not ignore was her need to look her best tonight. She wanted to make it hard for Dima to keep his eyes off her.

She looked once again at her nineties-inspired outfit.

The vintage jeans she'd picked up at a consignment shop from a top-label designer had strategic rips and aging, but what they did to her butt was amazing. Her rust-colored short T-shirt clung to her body, but it was saved from being too sexy for a family dinner by the blue plaid shirt she wore over it.

Her jewelry wasn't vintage, but she loved the statement pieces made by female entrepreneurs in Vietnam. The doorbell rang and she tucked her hair behind her ear out of habit.

She'd brushed her blond hair to a sheen of soft waves falling to her shoulders and refreshed her natural-toned makeup. Nothing more to do to get ready for this date.

Family dinner as a date. She almost smiled at that, but the sudden advent of nervous butterflies in her tummy kept the smile from fruition.

Jenna shut the door on her now messy room, forcing down the urge to ask Dima to wait while she straightened things up a little.

She hated leaving dishes in the sink or clothes on the bed or floor when she went out.

Dima himself waited on the other side of her door, and that brought the aborted smile out in full force.

"You could have just texted, and I would have come down," she chided.

He leaned in and kissed both her cheeks. "Not my style."

She returned the familiar Mirrusian greeting, her entire body lighting up as she pressed chaste kisses to his cheeks.

They were in the parking garage, walking toward the car, when he said, "I like those jeans. Very retro."

"Thank you." She looked back over her shoulder and noticed his attention was firmly on her backside. She smiled. "I like the way they fit."

"I do too." He said it in an undertone, but one of the security men made a sound like a stifled laugh.

Dima gave him a sardonic look but didn't seem embarrassed to be caught ogling her. Jenna was doing her own ogling, so she could hardly complain.

Dima wore a tight-fitting lightweight silk sweater and slacks cut to show off his gorgeous body.

He stepped around her and flicked a remote in his hand. The door on the passenger side of the high-end sports car opened. Black, of course, the car gleamed under the lights of the parking garage. Even with the powerful engine and sleek lines, no Mirrusian prince would go for a color as attention-grabbing as red.

Dinner with Dima's family was as fun as it usually was. Living in the same city, Emma and Jenna had become very good friends over the years. Jenna had learned to tolerate Konstantin, and she adored their two boys.

Emma was down-to-earth, just like Nataliya, her role as princess only part of who she was. She was an amazing artist and really involved mom. Not to mention head over heels in love with her husband, Prince Konstantin.

There was no accounting for taste. Sure, Konstantin was a pretty decent guy, but Jenna would probably never forgive him completely for treating Nataliya like he had.

He'd had his reasons, Emma being the biggest one, but Nataliya had nearly lost her family over her decision not to fulfill a contract Konstantin had no real intention of fulfilling either.

He might have lied to himself, but anyone who saw him with Emma would know he couldn't have married another woman and stuck it.

The boys, however, were adorable as ever, suckering Jenna into a game of hide-and-seek before dinner.

"Now, count to sixty and don't look."

"They want to see if you can figure out their latest hiding spot," Emma informed Jenna as the boys rushed away, being awfully light-footed for a twelve- and a seven-year-old.

She couldn't tell if they'd stayed on the main floor or gone up the mansion's staircase.

"I remember doing the same with my siblings." Jenna's heart panged as it always did when she thought of the years before they'd lost her brother. "My sister and I were always trying to outguess our older brothers."

"I thought you only had one brother," Emma said, her brow furrowed.

"I do. Now." They'd lost Matt when she was sixteen.

"I'm sorry for your loss." The words might be a cliché, but Emma's tone was filled with sincerity.

"Thank you. I never stop missing him, you know?"

"I never had siblings," Emma said softly. "I can imagine, though. I love Dima, Nikolai and Nataliya like siblings and I cannot imagine losing one of them, much less one of the children."

"The princes all experienced loss early." The queen had died, and it had probably been the beginning of the end of Prince Evengi's reign.

He'd abdicated to his adult son after a near fatal heart attack almost two decades ago.

His willingness to do so had always impressed Jenna. While Prince Evengi had been a king who ultimately had refused the idea of a constitutional monarchy, he was not a man who put tradition and royal duty above all else.

He'd preserved his own life for the sake of his children.

The fact he'd lived long enough to woo and then marry Nataliya's mother, the former countess, was just one more reason that choice had been a good one.

"He and Solomia are coming to visit next month," Emma said, showing their thoughts had traveled down a similar path. "Will you come for dinner again? I know they'll want to see you."

"Of course, but right now I think I need to go searching for your sons."

"They're going to be thrilled it took you this long to find them," Emma said with warm humor in her tone.

In fact, it took Jenna another several minutes of searching before she discovered the boys tucked into what she would have thought was an impossibly small space behind storage boxes in an under-stairs closet she'd peeked into twice before the third time going to the far back on a hunch.

She took their teasing over dinner about how poorly she'd done finding them in good humor.

Mikhail, especially, reminded her of Matt. Jenna doubted she could ever be angry or even annoyed with the twelve-year-old.

"You're a fabulous auntie, you know?" Emma said when the boys had left the table. "They adore when you come to visit."

"They do." Konstantin managed to infuse his tone with a surfeit of disbelief.

She made a face at him. "Your sons have good taste."

"They have never been treated to the edge of your tongue." Konstantin's expression said he wasn't particularly worried he had.

"Sharp-tongued? Our Jenna?" Dima teased. "I don't believe it."

"Yes, well, you weren't the prince expected to marry her best friend as the result of in her words, a draconian contract that any adult man with an ounce of respect for women would never have signed."

"I did say that." Jenna grinned cheekily. "And I stick by it."

"She signed it too."

"She was a teenager, and she was under pressure."

"So was I." It was an old argument, and the prince didn't seem to be taking it any more seriously than she was.

"You weren't a teen," Emma said. "But you were under pressure. I love your dad, bless his heart, but he knows how to administer a guilt trip."

"He's a professional at them," Dima agreed ruefully.

Konstantin nodded vehemently. "So, how have you remained single with no *draconian* contracts on your horizon?"

"That contract caused a lot of grief for you, Emma and his grandson, not to mention for Nataliya. It didn't take much to extract a promise from Father not to try anything of the like with me."

"I hear a *but* in your voice."

"But I have agreed to allow him and Solomia to introduce me to what he deems appropriate women."

Jenna's stomach plummeted, though she could not have said why. She wasn't looking for long-term with Dima, and she for sure didn't want to join the royal family for real.

Emma flicked a quick glance Jenna's way, looking a little worried, though Jenna didn't know why she would. "You agreed to let him matchmake for you?"

"Not matchmake, introduce. I have no intention of getting married anytime soon, and I'm definitely not going to start dating a woman of his choosing."

"Good luck with that," Konstantin said with a laugh.

"I'm hardly on the bubble to marry soon, being the youngest. In centuries past, I would have made a career out of the military or the church."

"Orthodox priests can marry."

"Indeed. However, none of our ancestors who became priests did so."

"Really?" Emma asked with interest. "I wonder why?"

"I would love to sit around and chat about our ancestors, but it's time to get back to my hotel."

"If you don't want to leave, I can run you home later," Emma offered Jenna.

"Or have a driver do so," Konstantin drawled sardonically.

Emma blushed. "We've been married seven years and still, I forget."

"That you are a princess?"

Jenna still remembered when news of Emma and her four-year-old son had rocked the royal family. It had been a hard time for Prince Konstantin, realizing that his own actions and those of someone he considered a friend had kept the woman he loved and the child he had not known about from him.

"And obscenely wealthy." Emma rolled her eyes. "There's something to be said for being a starving artist."

"There's something to be said for being married to your soul mate," Konstantin instantly countered.

Emma smiled. "I'm willing to be convinced."

"And on that note, we are out of here," Dima said, sounding a lot more like a younger sibling than a prince, or a business tycoon.

"Hmm, what are we doing here, I wonder?" Jenna mused, her voice laced with humor.

Dimitri turned off the sports car's powerful engine but left the ignition remote in the console for the valet. "You are just now asking?"

It had to have been obvious to her that he wasn't returning Jenna to her home within the first two turns of their drive.

"You could have been taking the scenic route." She gave him a droll look.

"I told you my plans earlier."

"You implied you had plans for seduction," she acknowledged just as the hotel staff opened her door and offered her a hand.

She turned and smiled up at the porter with pure innocence. "Thank you."

Shaking his head, Dimitri got out of the car and left security to deal with the parking instructions.

Two of his current team of four followed at a discreet distance as he led Jenna to the bank of elevators. They slipped inside the car with them, though, and his head bodyguard swiped the key card that allowed access to the penthouse floor of suites.

Jenna chatted with the security men on the way up, asking about their families, if they enjoyed traveling for their jobs. Dimitri would have put it down to the natural curiosity of a reporter, but genuine interest shone in her brown eyes.

Jenna cared about people.

Once they were in the penthouse, Jenna dropped her bag and shrugged out of her coat. Springtime weather in Seattle was mercurial, but one thing could be relied on, a drop in temperature after sunset.

Jenna showed her native Northwest roots by bringing along a jacket, even on a surprisingly warm and sunny spring day.

He took her coat and hung it over a chair while she looked around, taking in their surroundings.

"One thing I can say about your family. You all know how to travel in style."

He looked around the modern suite that was the size of his apartment while at university and shrugged. "The level of security we need comes with its own standard of luxury."

"Does it?" Her chocolate gaze mocked him.

"Tease me at your peril, lady."

"Oh, I am not one of those. I'm just a garden variety woman and happy to be so."

He stepped right into her personal space but did not reach out to touch her as he was itching to do. "I would never classify you as garden variety anything."

"Compliments? Already?"

"Compliments always." Jenna Beals was an amazing woman, and he'd always thought so.

She was a good friend to Nataliya, as close as any sister. There was no way that Jenna was the knowing source of the information leaks. Which left two possibilities: she was confiding in the wrong person, or she was being spied on somehow.

Tonight his security detail would be searching her home for listening devices while she was with him at his hotel. He would need to search her handbag.

It was highly unlikely her phone had been compromised. Guests who did not submit to the mobile phone security protocols at the palace had their devices locked in a secure vault that blocked all signals for the duration of their stay.

To his knowledge, Jenna had never refused to have her phones upgraded with the latest security software and checked on every visit to the palace.

"You've got a strange look on your face."

He gave himself a mental shake. "Do I? Are you sure it's not just the look of a man who wants to kiss you?"

Which he did. Even without his brother's request, Dimitri would have come looking for Jenna. His desire for her only grew as the years went by.

He'd never acted on it when they were both visiting the palace. It hadn't felt right, but then, he'd never taken a lover to the palace, much less taken one while staying there from among the guests.

Too much opportunity for scandal, and really? His family had already had enough of that. He and his brothers had each brought their own kind of notoriety to the royal house, and not in a good way.

Dimitri had no intention of featuring in the scandal rags again if he could help it.

"You're doing it again," Jenna said.

"What?"

"Thinking."

"How can you tell?" He was genuinely curious. Controlling his emotions and expressions had been taught to Dimitri from the cradle.

"You get this look."

"What look?"

She sighed in exasperation. "The one you just had on your face."

"I do not have it now?"

"No. Now you look irritated."

"Wow."

"What?"

"I am irritated." And she could tell. Unbelievable.

He had better control than that.

"Why?" she asked.

"I don't like the idea of being so easily read by someone," he said with more honesty than he would usually offer.

"Oh, well, I've known you a long time," she said consolingly. "It is inevitable I would learn your tells."

"If you say so." Even his brothers weren't that adept at reading Dimitri.

"What were you thinking about so hard?"

"You'd rather talk than kiss?" he asked, a little offended.

She rolled her eyes. "Are you saying we can't do both?"

That was not a denial she wanted to kiss him, and he took that as a win. "I was thinking about how my brothers and I have brought enough scandal to our family."

Which meant finding out how someone was mining Jenna for information was paramount. Especially now that Nataliya was pregnant again and *not* ready to go public with the knowledge.

"You can't be angry with Kon for not knowing about his son."

Dimitri gave a mental sigh. She really did want to talk.

And damn it, as much as he found it strange, he enjoyed their conversations enough to put off the kissing.

And other things.

For a little while anyway.

"No. Would you like something to drink?" He headed toward the wet bar.

"I'll take a whiskey."

"No white wine spritzer?" That seemed to be the drink du jour among the women in his family.

"If I were driving after, sure, but I plan on staying a while."

"You aren't nervous?" he asked, bothered that could be the case.

"Dutch courage, you mean?" She laughed as she kicked off her shoes, the sound going straight to his groin. "Not all. I learned to enjoy slow-sipping Scotch whiskey when I was on an assignment in Edinburgh."

"Edinburgh and fashion are not synonymous in my mind."

"Don't be a snob. Fashion isn't limited to New York, Milan and Paris, I promise you." She settled onto the sofa, her feet tucked up beside her.

Dimitri poured them both a scant shot of well-aged whiskey. He handed one to her before sitting beside her. "I'm learning all sorts of new things about you."

"I think before this night is over, you're going to know a lot of things you didn't." The look she gave him told him she wasn't talking about her preference in beverages.

Dimitri did nothing to stifle the smile that thought elicited. "I'm looking forward to it."

"So, if you don't blame Konstantin for the scandal he brought to the family, do you blame Nikolai?"

"I don't blame anyone. It is what it is."

"Really? You don't blame *anyone*?" Her tone was tinged with disbelief.

"You mean Tiana?" Nikolai's first wife had done damage to both his older brothers in her pursuit of what she wanted.

Or did not want.

Responsibility. Motherhood.

"She was a piece of work." Distaste showed on Jenna's lovely features. "I was actually thinking more about Galena."

Dimitri frowned. "I don't talk about her." His former fiancée was a part of his past he had no desire to revisit.

"Nataliya's dad has some blame for the months your family spent in the tabloids too," Jenna said, showing no signs she was bothered that he did not want to discuss Galena.

"He does, though Nikolai got out ahead of him with the media."

"Your brother is a smart man. He married Nataliya after all."

"Smartest thing he ever did," Dimitri readily agreed.

The woman who had been born into Volyarusian nobility made a damn fine queen.

"On the other hand, I thought my best friend had lost her mind when she agreed to marry a king."

Dimitri laughed. "They have two children and a country in common now."

"She wants more children. This pregnancy, she doesn't want it to be her last."

"You know she is pregnant?" he asked.

"Of course, I do. Who do you think she called first?"

"Her mother?"

Nataliya smile was wry. "Okay, yes, maybe. But of course she told me."

"You two are really close."

"I love her as much as I do my birth siblings."

"I cannot imagine trusting a friend as much as I do my brothers," he said truthfully.

"Not even the men you served with?"

Dimitri shook his head in negative without hesitation. "Trusting a man with your life is not the same as being able to trust him with your secrets."

"You have secrets, Your Highness? Do tell."

A much bigger laugh than he was used to allowing burst out of Dimitri. "Not a chance."

"Because I'm not family?"

"You're as much family as Nataliya and Emma." She might not be married into their family, but Jenna was definitely a part of it.

"You wouldn't share with them either, but you and Nataliya have been friends for years. She told me you used to text her when you were away at school."

"I did." He'd seen the Volyarusian as an imminent member of his family since she'd signed that crazy contract at the age of eighteen. "She convinced Nikolai and my father that the gap year I requested was a good idea."

"And still, you wouldn't tell her your secrets?"

"I don't make it a habit to confide in anyone."

"Not even your brothers?"

"Not about everything."

Hid dad came closest to being Dimitri's confidant, but even then, Dimitri had a habit of holding things back, for many reasons. The most important was that as great as his father was, the man had an agenda of seeing all his sons married, and Dimitri wasn't giving him any ammunition for salvos in that direction.

Dimitri had never shared with anyone all that he experienced in combat. The two men who had experienced it all with him had not survived their final mission.

"What about Galena? I'm not asking you to dissect your past relationship," she assured him before he could shut her down again. "I just want to know if you ever confided in her."

The name of his ex-fiancée did not bring warm, fuzzy feelings to Dimitri at the best of times. When he was sitting on the couch with the one woman he had wanted for years, it was like a bucket of ice water.

"What is this fixation you have on who I share my secrets with?"

"Because we all have to have someone, and it worries me that you don't."

That answer surprised him enough he blurted out, "You think a woman who cheated on me and eloped with another man while I was in hospital would have been a good candidate?"

Dimitri might be the youngest, but it had been a long time since anyone evinced that kind of worry over him. He would have hated it from someone else but found patience for it with Jenna.

She was just that kind of woman. Despite her sarcastic demeanor, she cared about everyone.

"Clearly not, but the fact you didn't trust the woman you asked to marry you says a lot."

He was not sure what she thought it said, but Dimitri was certain that right now, he wasn't interested in finding out. "I don't understand how we got sidetracked by this kind of heavy discussion."

This was not pre-kissing conversation. Not in his book.

"When you were just looking for a good night of bedroom gymnastics?" she teased, not sounding perturbed by the thought.

"A fantastic night, thank you."

Her smile was filled with the kind of heat he didn't mind getting burned by. "I could go for fantastic."

CHAPTER FOUR

HE REACHED OUT to do what he'd been wanting for a hell of a lot longer than he wanted to admit, and pulled her close, his body going from zero to Mach 1 in a single breath. "Fantastic it is."

She didn't wait for him to kiss her but leaned forward and pulled his head towards her at the same time. Her lips pressed against his, her body doing the same.

It was no tentative kiss, but pure sexual heat, their hands mapping each other's body with urgency he hadn't felt since he was still at university.

Sex was a necessary, delicious part of life.

This kind of sex made him feel like he *was* alive.

She climbed into his lap, spreading her thighs over his and kissing him with the kind of unfettered passion he'd only dreamed of finding in a lover.

Literally. He had dreamed about this woman, waking up hard and aching, craving just this kind of sensual abandon from her.

They didn't make it into the bedroom but stripped each other right there in the suite's sitting room. Her breasts were gorgeous and full, rosy-tipped peaks tempting him.

She cried out when he took one in his mouth and suckled, undulating her hips against him. He was steel hard and aching to be inside her. Rubbing his erection against her slick opening, up and down, but without shifting so he could penetrate.

He had to get a condom on. Now.

She gasped and jerked backward. "Condom," she gasped. "I've got one in my bag."

He didn't ask why. They'd both known how this night was going to end.

"Hurry," he urged.

She jumped up and rushed to her bag, and dug through it, tossing things with abandon onto the table. She lifted a strip of condoms in her hand. "Yes!"

"Bring it here," he demanded.

"Bossy." But she complied, crossing the room quickly.

He put his hand out. "Give it to me."

"I want to put it on you."

"If you do, it may be over before it begins." He would have been loath to admit that to someone else. Probably wouldn't have done so.

But he knew she wouldn't take it as weakness, or lack of sexual prowess. Not with how hot she was too.

She didn't. In fact, her dark gaze glowed with increased desire as she handed over one of the foil packets. "Do it."

"Who is bossy?" he teased to cover the tremble of his hand as he tore the packet open and pulled out the protection.

Even sliding it on himself made him groan. She climbed back onto his lap without preamble, arranging their bodies so the head of his prick kissed her slick entrance.

Using all of his self-control, his body taut with need, Dimitri waited for her to take him inside her.

Jenna shifted down and then forward, her body taking him in an increment at a time. She kept shimmying, making sexy noises that had him so close to coming he started reciting the Cyrillic alphabet backwards in his head.

Dimitri surged upward, pulling her down toward him, and he was fully seated inside her. They both groaned. "So good. Why is it so good with you?" she asked.

He had no answer. He only knew it was perfect.

They began a rhythm as old as time, their bodies surging together again and again. The sound of skin slapping against skin, panting and moans filled the air around them.

"Yes, harder!" She followed that demand with a word he'd never heard her say before, but one that felt very appropriate to the moment.

He obeyed, using his core and thigh muscles to piston in and out of her, helping her tilt her pelvis so he pressed against the spot inside her that made her scream. Over and over.

He was shouting too, promising they would both come soon, telling her she was perfect, and the sort of stuff he would never say in his right mind.

Suddenly she was convulsing around him, her climax nearly silent after very noisy sex. Her face was fixed in a rictus of pleasure that was one of the most beautiful things he'd ever seen. Then he was coming too, and his arms locked around her.

Too tight, but he couldn't make himself let go. He had to hold her as he came inside her for the first time.

She held him too, her own arms nearly as tight, her face pressing into his shoulder as they both shook with the aftershocks of pleasure.

He did not know how long they remained like that, but eventually he said, "That was pretty good for round one."

Her laughter rippled through her and around his flesh still inside her, bringing round two closer than it had been a moment before.

"You're good for a second time?" she asked with a smile. "It's a good thing. That one was pretty darn fast."

"Neither one of us was slowing down."

"No, we weren't."

He was careful to hold on to the condom as she disengaged.

She stood up and gave a rueful look to their clothes strewn around. "We didn't even make it to the bed."

"That sofa worked well." It had in fact been just the right angle and height to make their frenzied lovemaking work.

She grinned. "Maybe we'll have to use it again."

"I like that idea, but right now, how about the Jacuzzi?" he offered. He'd had dreams about making love to her in water more than once. Not that he was admitting that out loud.

Wet dreams were not something adult men suffered from. Unless they met a woman like Jenna.

"Your suite has its own hot tub?" she asked now. "Swank."

"As good as. Both the rooftop pool and hot tub are reserved for my private use while I am here."

"I thought this hotel had a pool on the ground floor."

"They do."

"And a rooftop pool?" she asked, heading into the bedroom.

He got up on legs that felt just a little shaky. "Only for guests on the penthouse level."

"Sucks to be another guest while you're here, then," she said from the bathroom.

She came out wearing one of the white Turkish robes provided by the hotel and carrying another. She held it out.

"My security staff are using the other penthouse." He shrugged on the robe. "They can make use of the pool area when I am not."

"Really?" she asked a little skeptically.

"Why ask that? You know how my family see our staff."

"As valuable. Yes, I know, but you told them they could use the pool."

"Not tonight. I thought you might enjoy a naked swim."

"Is that safe?" She couldn't be too concerned, wearing the robe and nothing else with every evidence of being willing to go with him to the roof.

"Hotel security cameras have been disabled on this floor and the rooftop for the duration of my stay," he assured her. "My own security measures have been installed."

"Sounds like a lot of work."

Sometimes it surprised him the things *she* didn't know about how his family lived. "You realize that in addition to being ruling royalty, my family is worth billions of dollars?"

"Um…" The look of consternation on her features said she hadn't really ever given it a lot of consideration. "I just thought Nataliya's security was because she was queen, you know?"

"Certainly, that's part of it."

They took a private set of stairs up to the roof. Half the pool was enclosed in a pool house, the other half exposed to the elements. The hot tub was outside, steam coming off the water in the springtime chill.

Lights bathed the rooftop oasis in a gentle low light that did not detract from the view of Seattle at night.

"It's beautiful up here."

"And all ours for the night."

Jenna was having trouble believing she was here. Well, not here exactly. As impressive as this private rooftop pool area was, she'd been to some pretty amazing places in her life. Not least of which since her BFF had married a king.

But Jenna had never expected to act on the attraction

she felt for Dima. Yet, here they were, practically naked and planning more sexy times in this private oasis.

"I have to say, Dima, if you set out to impress me, you succeeded."

"Good to know." He pulled her around and slid his hand inside her robe, no lack of confidence in this man, despite their age difference. "Now, tell me, was it the amazing sex downstairs, or is it the pool that's done it?"

His hands on her naked skin were distracting her, so it took Jenna a second to answer. "The pool would be nothing but a fun diversion without the incredible sex that came before."

He didn't reply with words but leaned down and took her mouth in a delicious kiss while undoing the tie on her robe, and then slid it off her shoulders. She let it fall in a pool around her feet. There was something incredibly decadent about being naked and out in the open air, content in the knowledge that no one could see them.

She tugged at his robe, wanting skin against skin again.

He complied without breaking the kiss, pulling her body flush with his when his robe had joined hers around their feet. Dima's strong hands cupped her backside, and he lifted. Jenna took the hint and hopped up, wrapping her legs around his hips.

It put her most intimate flesh against his, and she pressed against him, reveling in the bliss of having his hardness pressed against her clitoris, that bundle of nerves that gave so much pleasure. It wasn't enough, but it was a lot.

He made a growly sound deep in his throat, and she reveled in that too.

She'd reduced the urbane prince to his primal nature, and Jenna loved knowing it.

He started walking, but she paid no attention to where

they were going, her entire being focused on the kiss and the press of their naked bodies.

When her feet dipped into water, she gasped against his lips. A second later, the lower half of her body was in the lukewarm water.

The pool was heated, but it felt cool against her heated skin, and she gasped again, breaking the kiss. "What are you doing?"

"You need to ask? Really?"

She looked around them at the water that was now brushing against the underside of her breasts. "You want to go for a swim?"

"Not exactly, though we could certainly do that later." His smile was nothing short of devilish.

"Then what?" No way was he thinking of sexcapades in the water. Was he?

"This."

This was hands sliding over her body slickly, the water making the caresses feel different. *This* was him seducing her body with every wet touch, every slide of his limbs against hers under the water.

"Come, lie back and float. I promise you will like it."

Jenna allowed herself to be maneuvered onto her back to float, her wet nipples peaking with near painful arousal in the night air.

It was the strangest feeling to have part of her body exposed to the air and the rest in the water, but all open to his touch. Sensual in a way she'd never experienced before.

Jenna had had her fair share of lovers, but none had ever been this confident, this adventurous.

Dima slid his hands over her body, touching every dip and crevice, trailing his fingers with as much sensual care over her calves as he did her breasts. When he leaned down to take a nipple in his mouth, Jenna had to bite back a cry.

The naughty look he gave her said he knew exactly how hard it was for her to keep it down.

"I should be touching you too," she said, not sure she really believed it.

This felt too good.

"Believe me, I get all the pleasure I need touching you like this."

That was a heady thought, so Jenna went with it, relaxing in the water, letting her body float as he wanted. She had no idea how long she floated like that, with him touching her and telling her how sexy and beautiful she was, but at some point he'd moved them so the side of the pool was right there.

Dima ran his hands up her arms until their fingers meshed, and then he moved hers to the side of the pool. "Hold on."

"Don't drown me," she managed to tease.

"Never."

He glided through the water until he was between her legs, his hard sex pressing against her entrance. Dima stayed like that for several seconds, as if he was entranced by the moment.

Or waiting for her to beg.

She almost did just that, or at least demanded he enter, when she remembered protection.

"Condom!" She was proud of herself for remembering in her current state of intense arousal, if supremely frustrated for the necessity.

He cursed but did not shift away. "Are you on birth control?"

She knew what he was really asking and that he wouldn't do so if it wasn't safe.

"I have an IUD," Jenna offered without compunction. "But I don't do sex without condoms."

Never. Not once.

He gave her an unfathomable look. "I don't either."

She took those words in, let the implication settle deep inside her. He was asking for something with her he'd never had with another woman.

They were both so turned on that to stop would *hurt*, but neither was out of control. This was a decision they were both making with their brains as well as their bodies.

A decision she wanted to make. They weren't making promises. They'd both been clear from the start where this was going.

Nowhere serious. They were friends. With benefits.

Jenna had never actually had an arrangement like this with a man, but it was the only one she *could* have with a prince.

Maybe it was their longtime friendship. Maybe it was knowing he was part of her BFF's family, but Jenna wasn't worried about breaking her ironclad rule for Dima. She absolutely trusted him not to be putting her at risk.

She let her thighs float further apart in the water, the invitation obvious. "I'm safe."

"I never doubted it." His eyes were dark with need, his body rigid with control.

"Okay."

"You are sure?" he asked, though the sexual strain showed in how tightly he held his body, in how hard he was.

"Yes."

"Good." He pressed forward inside her, his hard flesh stretching hers, making room for himself in her body and somewhere deep in her heart.

Not that she was ever going to acknowledge that last bit.

Her body was buoyed by the water as he controlled the depth and speed of his thrusts. She had no hope of meeting him. Every time she tried to move, her hands would lose their grip, or her body would shift in the water, doing the opposite of what she'd intended.

He gripped her hips. "Just let it happen, Jenna. It will be good."

She was pretty sure *good* was a huge understatement. Trusting him to give her the blissful stimulation she needed, she concentrated on keeping her body relaxed and floating while he controlled their joining.

Sometime later, as she climaxed in wave after wave of pleasure, she had to admit he'd been right.

She loved it.

His shout as he came said he did too, and that he wasn't nearly as worried as she was about being overheard. Though who she thought was going to hear them, she wasn't sure. Only, rooftop or not, they *were* outside.

Dima carried her to the showers, and they washed each other's bodies, kissing in the way that lovers do after mind-shattering orgasms.

When Jenna found herself sliding into bed beside Dima, she acknowledged, if only to herself, that she was breaking another rule. She didn't sleep with men she wasn't committed to.

And again, she wanted to.

Dimitri waited until Jenna was sleeping soundly before sliding quietly from the bed. He went out to the living area on silent feet, pulling the door shut behind him. He found her purse, most of the contents still spilled out on the table.

He started going through it all, item by item, examining each for any kind of surveillance device. He wasn't actually expecting to find something in her handbag. It didn't make sense to plant a device in something Jenna switched out to compliment her mood and outfit.

So when he discovered a sophisticated micro listening device incorporated into the design of a portable phone stand, he cursed quietly in shock.

Well, that explained a lot. Jenna used the stand when she video chatted with Nataliya; Dimitri had seen her do it. Even when they were at the palace together, they would call each other when Nataliya's schedule allowed for a call but not to break away long enough to get together in person.

The Volyarusian palace covered three city blocks, certainly not a few seconds' walk from one area to another.

He'd always thought the two women's closeness was special, and it infuriated him that someone would use it against them.

As glad as he was to find the device, Dimitri knew Jenna was going to be devastated when he told her someone had been spying on her.

He pulled out the remaining items in Jenna's bag, examining each one just as closely as before. He could not assume there was only one device. Although he found nothing.

He then examined the bag, and his anger grew when he found another device inserted under a buckle on the shoulder strap. How many of her accessories had been compromised like this?

Whoever had done this was serious about gathering intel on the royal family through Jenna.

"What are you doing?" Jenna's voice startled him.

He should have heard her get out of bed. What was wrong with him that he hadn't?

"You woke up," he said rather inelegantly as he turned to face her.

"You weren't there." She frowned, like that wasn't what she meant to say. "Why is everything scattered like that? I know I pulled stuff out earlier, but not all of it." She blinked, sounding a little out of it and very confused, her beautiful brown eyes looking unfocused.

His body and brain were at cross-purposes as he struggled with his instant, nearly overwhelming response to the sight of her tousled hair and naked body. She looked like she'd just come from bed, and he knew she had. His bed. That knowledge was doing crazy things to his libido.

"Let's talk about it in the morning, *milaya moy.* You're tired, and there are much more pleasurable things we can do with the night than talk."

Jenna's body shifted subtly, but suddenly she was alert and not looking nearly as sleepy. "What exactly do we need to talk about? And when did I become your *darling*?"

He'd called her *darling*? Dimitri played his words back in his own mind and realized not only had he called her *milaya*, but he'd added the possessive *moy.* My darling. Shrugging off how uncharacteristic that was for him, he answered the easier question first. "I'd say calling the woman I had sex with twice tonight *darling* might be expected."

She bit her lip but nodded. "Okay, but that doesn't tell me what this serious thing is we need to talk about."

"You are so sure it's serious?"

"Yes, or you would have simply taken me back to bed while explaining what you were doing rummaging through my—"

He put his hand up and shook his head before she could mention exactly what he'd been doing. At the same time, he cursed inwardly. He'd mentioned them having sex. If the person spying on Jenna was monitoring, they would know it too.

Damn it.

But that wasn't as bad as the conversation that was coming, because it was going to hurt her.

He was tempted to sigh, but princes did not expose their thoughts so easily. However, internally Dimitri wished he could avoid what he knew was coming. He hated thinking Jenna was going to be hurt by the spy's actions.

"If you want to talk, grab a robe," he informed her. "You'll be far too much of a distraction otherwise."

She gave him a look, but retreated to the bedroom, coming back seconds later, tying her robe. He was closing the door on the room's safe, the handbag and phone stand tucked safely inside in the lead compartment that would not allow any electronic transmission.

Jenna threw the robe she'd had tucked under her arm at him. "Cover yourself. The same goes."

Stifling the reply he wanted to give, Dimitri slipped into the robe, surprisingly resentful that he had to deal with family business before they could return to the bedroom. Dimitri never resented doing his duty.

Jenna was giving him a searching look, her brows drawn together. "Why did you put those things in the safe?"

"Did you buy that phone holder, or was it a gift?" he asked, rather than answering.

"It was a gift. Now tell me why you tucked my purse and phone stand away like the crown jewels." She spoke more forcefully, her intention of getting answers clear in her tone.

Finessing around the subject wasn't going to do either of them any favors. "There were listening devices in both."

"What do you mean listening devices?"

"High-tech micro-sized microphones that transmit to a receiver."

"I know what a listening device is." She gave him a look that said she wasn't impressed. "I just don't understand how you're telling me there was one on my purse and phone stand."

"Someone has been spying on you."

Jenna's lovely features leached of color. "No. That's not possible."

"Yes."

"But how could you know?"

No doubt Konstantin would expect Dimitri to lie, but Dimitri knew that Jenna wasn't going to put her BFF at any more at risk than the rest of them would. She wasn't going to go calling Nataliya the moment he and she were done talking.

So he told her about the leaks and Konstantin's certainty they were somehow coming from her.

"You're saying Prince Konstantin thought *I* was leaking stuff to the press, about *your* family and Mirrus Global?" Jenna asked in a flat tone he'd never heard from her before.

"He wasn't convinced it was you personally, but yes, he knew it was coming via you. Somehow. And it did," he pointed out. She couldn't be offended at the truth.

Jenna was far too pragmatic a woman to be that dramatic.

"*You* thought I was the leak, and you slept with me?" Her tone wasn't flat now, but near shouting.

"Clearly not. I wouldn't have been searching your handbag if I did, or have my security searching your apartment." What did she think? That he didn't know her at all?

"You have security men searching my apartment?" she asked, sounding even angrier, certainly not mollified by that news. "How did they get in?"

He just looked at her.

"Fine, they have their ways." She stared around her like she was horrified, and having a difficult time taking his words in. "I can't believe you've had strangers pawing through my stuff without even telling me first."

Jenna was focusing on the wrong issue here, and it surprised him.

"They aren't strangers," he assured her. "It's my personal security team. You've met them before. You talk to them."

He didn't mention he couldn't risk telling her if she was the actual leak. Her current reaction indicated that wouldn't go over well. At all.

She was responding with unexpected emotion. He'd thought she would be hurt, but because she was being spied on, not because he was trying to figure out what was going on.

"Oh, that makes it so much better." Her tone said the exact opposite.

"Jenna, if you just look at this situation rationally, you'll see I took the best course of action."

"No. No. No." She shook her head. "You are not standing there telling me you had sex with me to figure out if I was some sort of spy and that it was the *best* you could come up with."

"Of course not. I had sex with you because I want you. You want me too."

"You used it as a diversion to get me out of my apartment."

He couldn't deny that, but it was not the whole truth, or even the most salient truth. What could he say that would not dig him deeper in this pit he had never thought he would find himself in?

"You and I were both done dancing around this attraction between us."

The expression on Jenna's face said those were not the right words.

CHAPTER FIVE

JENNA FELT LIKE ants were crawling along her skin.

Dima thought the fact that they wanted each other justified him using sex to keep her out of her apartment while it was searched?

She wanted to throw up.

"You don't look well. Sit down and I'll get you a brandy. I knew finding out you were being spied on was going to upset you." He offered his hand, like he really expected her to take it.

"I haven't even started to process that," she assured him. "I'm furious and hurt that you used sex between us as a tool." She spelled it out in case he still didn't get it. "I trusted you."

She'd thought they were friends. Friends could trust each other.

His dark brows drew together. "You can still trust me."

In what universe? "No. I can't."

"Don't be dramatic, Jenna. Nothing about tonight has changed other than I had to give you some upsetting news."

"You're talking about someone supposedly spying on me."

"Yes, of course. And there's no *supposedly* about it. I found two listening devices. I haven't heard from my team yet, but if your bag was bugged, chances are other frequently used accessories are as well."

Stomach acids suddenly too unruly to control, Jenna spun and rushed toward the en suite. She was retching into the sink moments later, trying hard not to actually throw up.

A cold cloth was placed gently on the back of her neck while a hand rubbed her back in a soothing motion.

The urge to elbow the arrogant prince away from her was almost overwhelming. "Don't touch me," she gritted out.

He stepped away and left the bathroom. Both grateful and angry that he'd left so easily, Jenna bathed her face with cool water and then dried it as she fought to get her feelings and body's response to Dima's revelations under control.

How could he have used her like that?

How could either he or Konstantin think she would ever knowingly betray their family's trust? Was Nikolai in on this?

These were people she'd considered family for more than half a decade.

And they thought she could betray a woman as close as a sister?

Jenna would never hurt Nataliya, and every single one of those arrogant, distrusting royals should know it.

Equally to the point, she was a fashion editor, not a tabloid reporter. Did they really think all journalists were the same?

Intent on finding her clothes and getting dressed, Jenna turned around and nearly ran into Dima. He was holding a brandy snifter with a good inch of amber liquid in it. "Drink this. It will help."

Ignoring him, she maneuvered around Dima without

touching him and went in search of her clothes. They were scattered around the living area, and she grabbed each item with jerky movements, muttering to herself about untrusting, arrogant *jerks*.

"I did trust you. That is why I have my people searching your apartment."

She spun to face him, fury and hurt a maelstrom inside her. "Trust? You call that trust? If you trusted me, you would have told me what was going on."

He looked utterly shocked by the idea. Like he'd never even considered it. "I did tell you."

"When I caught you going through my purse, which, by the way, is considered a massive breach of trust by some women." Having grown up with a mother who routinely sent her children searching through her purse for everything from lunch money to allergy meds, Jenna wasn't one of them.

But that didn't make the fact any less true.

He managed to look a little uncomfortable at that reminder. "I apologize if that caused offense."

"Are you kidding me? First, that is a supremely lame apology. Second, you didn't just offend me, Your Highness. You hurt me!"

"That was not my intention. You must know that."

"No, I do not know that. I don't think you considered my feelings at all, to be honest, and that makes your *intentions* worth this." She snapped her fingers, signifying *nothing*.

"I planned to tell you everything in the morning." He spoke with exaggerated patience.

"Talking to me like you are trying to explain a complicated concept to a toddler is *not* digging you *out* of the pit you made." She glared at him, wishing she could at least singe his perfectly cut hair with the heat of her anger.

Who looked that good just climbing out of bed?

Jenna knew she didn't. Her hair was a mess, her makeup completely lost to their time in the shower and pool after.

So not the point, she reminded herself. Who cared how she looked to the Neanderthal standing in front of her?

"No, that's an insult to Neanderthals," she said aloud. "They were supposed to be intelligent and resourceful. You are a spoiled, distrusting *prince*."

"Being a prince is not a bad thing."

"You just keep believing that, Your Highness."

"Stop calling me Your Highness. I don't like it."

"I give this—" she paused and snapped her fingers again "—for what you like."

"You are very angry."

"And hurt." Jenna wasn't one of those people who thought hiding emotional pain made her stronger.

If someone hurt you, they should know it. If they *liked* that they hurt you, they had no business in any part of your life. Ever. At all.

Dima winced. "I am truly sorry I hurt you."

"That, at least, is a more sincere apology, but I don't forgive you, because you thought it was an okay thing to do. You *still* think it was acceptable to use sex as a tool of expedience and to investigate me behind my back." She deflated, her pain and disillusion overtaking her anger. "Not to mention the fact that you, or your brothers, could even suspect me of betraying Nataliya's confidence."

"I do not suspect you." His voice rang with truth, but it was way too little, too late.

"Well, certainly not now that you found the bugs." She shook her head. "You and Konstantin thought I could betray Nataliya. Does Nikolai?"

The expression on his features answered before he spoke. "I am sure he does not honestly believe it, but we had to be sure."

"You said you were sure before you searched my purse."
Had he been lying?

"I was. Just as I'm sure neither of my brothers genuinely believed you could be culpable."

She shook her head again. "It doesn't matter."

Done talking about something that could not be changed
and hurt too deeply for her to process in a matter of minutes, she went back into the bedroom, shutting the door
behind her.

Jenna dressed as quickly as she could, leaving her jewelry off. She stared down at it in her hand and realized she
couldn't just tuck it into her purse as she'd planned. Her
purse was locked in the suite's safe. She went in search of
something she could use to gather her possessions to take
with her and found a leather satchel.

Opening it, she found some files. Most were clearly
business files, and she took a second to wonder why Dima
didn't use a locked briefcase. But then all thoughts of
locked briefcases and better security flew from her mind
as she found a dossier on herself.

It was thorough, she'd give him that. It listed her entire
family, even her deceased brother. Not that Matt was a secret, but Jenna didn't often talk about his loss. Earlier that
evening with Emma had been an anomaly.

Every coworker, friend and acquaintance was listed as
well as the names of the men she'd dated in the past year
and a half, with short backgrounds on each.

She discovered one of the men she'd dated had lied
about his job and marital status. Divorced rather than never
married. The lies didn't surprise her. She'd felt like that
guy was off somehow. Not genuine. Her gut had been right.

So why hadn't it warned her about Dima?

That he could use her like this?

A peremptory knock sounded. "Are you coming back out?" Dima asked through the door.

It would serve him right if she didn't and left him to sleep on the sofa.

But Jenna was not a petty person. Never had been.

She marched over to the door and unlocked it, pulling it wide to glare up at the sneaky prince. "I found your file on me."

"You went through my things?" he asked, sounding and looking outraged.

That made her laugh. If it was more cynical than humorous, who could blame her? "Really? That's what you're going with?"

"There was no need. You could have asked, and I would have told you anything you wanted to know."

"I could say the same, though now, not so much. But I didn't go looking for answers to questions I'm not asking. I needed something to put the stuff from my purse in."

"So you decided to confiscate my briefcase?"

"Why doesn't it have a lock? For a family worried about security, yours is really lax."

"Without a lock, it looks less important, and since I travel with a security detail, locking my files away is unnecessary."

"Until you bring the wrong woman to your bed."

"You are not the wrong woman. You would do nothing with what you found in there."

"You're so sure about that?"

"You know I am. I was before I searched for surveillance devices, and I'm only more so now."

"Sure. I believe you." She let her tone tell him she actually felt the opposite.

His gorgeous face creased in a frown. "I don't bring

other women to my home or personal suite when I'm traveling. They do not have access to sensitive information."

"So? Am I supposed to feel special?"

"I don't know. How you feel is up to you, but I will tell you that you are special."

She made a disbelieving sound.

"Jenna, you are part of our family."

"I used to think that too, but family members don't spy on each other."

"I was not spying on you."

"What would you call it?"

"Trying to find out how information was passing through you to someone else."

"Behind my back. That *is* spying."

He walked over to the pile of files she had discarded and picked them up, then laid them on the bed in front of her. "You see these files?"

"I could hardly miss them."

"Usually I find your sarcasm sexy, but right now I could do with a little less of it."

"I could do without everything that happened tonight, to be honest." There was no sarcasm in her tone.

His grimace said he understood she'd meant every word. "I am sorry. Perhaps I should have talked to you about what Konstantin had discovered."

"What exactly is that?"

"I will get to that in a minute. Look at those files."

"Why?"

"Because I trust you."

"And looking at your business files proves that, how?" she asked, curious despite herself.

"They pertain to the biggest deal I have ever put together for Mirrus Global. You can read them cover to cover. I know you won't do anything with the information."

Again, despite herself, Jenna was impressed. Not that she was going to admit it, but the offer would have shocked her before tonight's events. She was more shocked now that she knew somebody was leaking information about his family.

"How did you find out someone was leaking information about the family?"

"It isn't just about the family. It's about Mirrus Global too." He went on to tell her what Konstantin had put together and brought to him.

"Why didn't he just approach me?"

"He was worried asking you would offend you and that you would vent to Nataliya and upset her."

"And right now, any kind of stress is not a good idea for her, but how did he not realize I'm fully aware of that? I wouldn't vent to Nataliya about anything that might upset her right now."

This seemed to sink in. "You are right. We both made a bad call even entertaining the thought you might."

"But not that *I* might be the leak?" she demanded, angry all over again.

"The leaks always coincided with you and Nataliya visiting each other or having a video call."

"We video call at least twice a month." It had been hard to adjust to her BFF not being available for daily chats like they used to have, but they texted almost every day still. "That seems like a pretty long stretch to causation."

"We were right. Someone is spying on you," he pointed out, like that made everything okay.

And just like that, she was done. Done with this conversation. Done with tonight. She just wanted to go home and be alone. Jenna needed time to process all this.

Only she couldn't go home, could she? "Has your team contacted you yet?"

"Yes. While you were getting dressed and ransacking my room for a handbag replacement."

"You just keep harping on that. It will remind us both what double standards you have."

He let out a sigh, and she stared at him in shock. She wasn't sure she'd ever heard Dima make such a *human* sound. Although she found it surprisingly easy to read his expression when others seemed to find him rather stoic, he did not express emotions with the typical sounds others made.

No surprised laughter, sighs or even grunts of annoyance from him.

He was too polished.

"I was teasing you, but clearly my timing was bad. It is not my intention to propagate a double standard."

"You sound pretty formal for a man who was inside my body only a few hours ago."

"As you have pointed out so many times, I am a prince."

"But not a robot." She shook her head. "Never mind. I want to leave, but I need to know if it is okay for me to return home."

"My security team would like time to try to trace the listening devices back to their source."

"That's not necessary. My assistant ordered the phone stand and delivered it to me. She has access to a lot of my accessories, like the purse I was using tonight, because designers gift them in hopes they'll be featured in the magazine. Skylar is the conduit for all swag that comes to me."

"If she's the one, it shouldn't take much to find out, but we can't assume that she is guilty because of proximity."

But it was okay to assume that Jenna had been guilty because of *her* proximity? She didn't bother pointing out yet another flaw in his brothers' and his thinking.

"I just want to go home."

"If you will not stay here with me, please consider allowing me to get you a room in the hotel. If you give me a list of things you need, the security team can gather them for you."

She'd planned to stay the night, but now she wanted anything but.

"Fine. Get a room for me sorted and my things delivered. I'll text a list of what I want you can forward to your security people. I assume it will all be checked for any more bugs."

Jenna did her best to ignore Dima's presence beside her as she made her way to the room she would use for the night. He'd insisted on escorting her, and she had simply not been willing to argue. The sooner she got to her room, the sooner she could shut the door on him.

"I would feel better if you slept in my suite." His tone was supremely patient.

She didn't bother to respond. Jenna had no desire to spend any more time arguing with the arrogant prince.

They reached her door, and she stepped forward to swipe the key card that had been delivered by the helpful hotel staff.

"Jenna," he said, his tone now tinged with exasperation. "Are you just going to ignore me?"

She turned and glared up at him. "Yes." Then she stepped into the room and shut the door on his too handsome face.

She flipped the security lock, although she was sure his security people would be there shortly with her things. She stared around the room, not at all surprised that it was not a standard single, but a suite.

Albeit much, much smaller than the penthouse suite she'd just left, it had a living room and a bedroom, and presumably a bathroom through the open door beyond. There was even a tiny kitchenette area, though why she would need one for a single night's stay she could not imagine.

For that matter, the living area was surplus to requirements. Jenna just needed a bed and a few hours of privacy to sleep.

Her knees started to wobble, and she stumbled to the sofa, plopping down.

Someone had been spying on her for at least a year, and despite Dima's refusal to *jump to conclusions*, Jenna was pretty sure she knew who it was.

Listening to her phone conversations, listening to her meetings, maybe even when she talked to herself in her apartment when she cleaned or brainstormed a layout, as she was wont to do. It all felt so icky, like slime was dripping from the edges of her life.

Typically, Dima had only looked at it in terms of his family, but Jenna had access to fashion concepts sometimes months before they were made public. People and businesses who had trusted her with their time-sensitive information could have been scooped because of her, and she had no idea.

She remembered the debacle last year when an established design label who were notoriously unimaginative had come out with a brand-new line. It had all but mirrored the one a new designer had shared with Jenna in hopes of getting a spread in her magazine for its launch.

The established house had brought their line out two weeks before the new designer.

The designer had accused Jenna of revealing her designs. Jenna had denied it, of course. She'd known she'd done no such thing.

Not only had the designer's new line been stolen, but her reputation had been damaged because she'd come for someone who everyone knew was trustworthy. Jenna's reputation was longer-standing and unassailable.

It had been a mess.

And now? How could she not wonder if she had in fact been the source of the leak?

That designer had lost her startup money and been forced to go back to designing for someone else.

Jenna had felt bad for her, even when she thought she hadn't been responsible. Now?

The guilt lay like an anvil in her gut.

As horrible as it was to be spied on, knowing that nothing confidential she'd worked on the past year had been safe was even worse. Other people had been hurt because of her.

She remembered how Nataliya had felt when news of her miscarriage was leaked ahead of the planned announcement. Nataliya and Nikolai had just wanted time to grieve in peace, but that had been stolen from them.

Because someone had access to Jenna.

Tears burned Jenna's eyes, but she refused to let them fall. The security people would deliver her stuff soon, and she didn't want to be caught crying like an infant.

A confident knock on the door sounded. She swiped at her eyes and went to open the door.

Swinging it open, she put her hand out to take her bag. "Thank you, I…"

Her voice trailed off when she realized Dima stood there, not his security person. And he wasn't holding a suitcase.

She frowned. "What do you want, Your Highness?"

"Damn it." He reached out as if to touch her, but she stepped back. "You've been crying. I knew I shouldn't leave you alone."

"Go away."

"You don't need to be alone right now."

She stared at him. "Are you for real? I mean, as arrogant as you can be, how can you not see that the last person I would want comfort from right now is you?"

"Be honest, Jenna. You aren't going to look for comfort from anyone. You're used to being the strong one."

He was right. As the oldest surviving sibling, she'd always considered it her job to carry the emotional burdens for her loved ones, not the other way around.

Knowing he was right and acknowledging it were two different things, however. "If you think you know me so well, why didn't you know that having sex with me as an expedient would hurt me?"

Taking advantage of the space she'd created stepping back from him, he moved into her room, shutting the door behind him.

He met her gaze, his own gray one steady. "It wasn't expedience. It was desire." His lips tilted on one side in a wry look. "The timing could have been better."

"Really? You think maybe?" Jenna retreated further, once again sitting on the sofa, the coffee table between them.

"Yes." He had the grace to look discomfited. "Jenna, *milaya moy*, I know this is hard on you. I didn't intend to make it harder."

That *my darling* hit her on the raw, taking what was left of her patience. "You need to go back to your suite, Your Highness. I am tired, and I'm going to bed."

"Your things will be arriving any minute."

"Good."

"Jenna—"

"I mean it, Prince Dimitri. Go away."

"I'm not the one who spied on you," he pointed out.

"Aren't you? What do you call going through my bag? Having your people scour my apartment behind my back?"

"Protecting you, as I am doing my best to protect the rest of my family, our company and our country."

"Protecting me?" she asked, disbelief coursing through her like waves crashing on the beach.

Cold and powerful.

He made an impatient gesture with his hand. "As much as it bothers me that someone has used you to get information on my family and company, I'm sure it has occurred to you that other areas of your life have been exposed as well."

"Don't pretend you care." She'd assumed he hadn't even considered that aspect.

"I do care, *milaya*."

"Enough with the Russian endearments." More than enough. She could not hear that word one more time without bursting into tears, and she had no idea why, but she wasn't going to pretend to herself she had a better hold on her emotions than she did. "It's not as cute as you seem to think it is."

"I am not trying to be *cute*."

"At this point, I cannot figure out what you are trying to be."

Another knock sounded on her door. This one a lot quieter, and Jenna had to shake her head that she'd thought the earlier confident and demanding one had been anyone other than Dima.

She went to get up to answer, but the prince beat her to it, opening the door and taking possession of her bag with minimal words.

"I can answer my own door," she pointed out.

He gave her a look that questioned why she felt the need to point that out. "Have I implied otherwise?"

"Never mind. Dima, I'm tired, and now my things are here. I want to go to bed."

"Yes, of course." But he made no move to relinquish her bag. "I do not want to leave you alone."

"I spend most nights alone."

"Tonight is not most nights."

No, it had been the best sex of her life followed by some awful news. Not that it competed with the worst news of her life, but learning Dima had used sex with her for his own ends and that she'd been spied on hurt all around.

She just wanted time to herself to lick her wounds, but the dense man seemed to think she needed company more. *His* company.

He put her suitcase down in the bedroom, coming back out immediately, his expression unhappy. Not something he would be happy to learn he expressed. He was so proud of his ability to hide his emotions.

All the princes were.

It was a thing.

A weird, royal thing.

She sat in silence, waiting for him to leave.

He stopped just before he reached the door and turned to face her again, his expression intent. "Sex between us was inevitable."

In that moment, she would have given anything to deny those words, but she couldn't. "Maybe, but it didn't have to happen tonight."

He inclined his head, like she'd made a point. "I am used to doing what I think is best."

"Arrogant."

"Probably."

"Good night, Your Highness."

He winced, as he'd done every time she used the title.

She would figure out what that meant later, after she'd gotten some sleep. Maybe.

"Good night, Jenna. I will see you tomorrow."

"No."

"We have to discuss a plan for going forward."

"Call me." There was no reason they had to meet face-to-face.

While her mobile phone was still locked in his safe, he could call the phone in her hotel room, or her work phone. Hopefully, her cell phone would be cleared and returned to her soon regardless.

By security.

She wasn't sure when she'd be ready to see any of the brothers face-to-face again, but tomorrow would not be it.

CHAPTER SIX

THE NEXT MORNING, Jenna got into her office two hours before anyone else was expected.

She put her things away in her office and then stood staring around, wondering if there were bugs in here too. Refusing to worry about it, she went back out into the main area and began searching her assistant Skylar's cubicle.

When Jenna found extra copies of a photo shoot, she didn't immediately excuse it as explainable as she once would have. How easy had it been for Skylar to pilfer information and pass it on for profit?

Jenna wasn't the only one on staff who assumed the best about people, particularly those working for them. An attitude of trust and empowerment was built into the magazine's employment culture.

The knowledge that that had been tainted and taken advantage of made Jenna really angry. Not all media companies valued those things, and she'd always been proud to work for one that did.

With renewed determination, she continued her search. Even with righteous anger fueling her, she was unable to dismiss the similarities in her own behavior to Dima's.

Jenna had convinced herself that Skylar was responsible based on circumstantial evidence. However, they were *not* friends, and she had a lot less reason to trust the other woman than the Merikovs had to trust Jenna.

Not finding anything else suspicious in the cubicle, she went to her own office and started looking for bugs. She didn't think she'd recognize anything for what it was, but she *would* know what wasn't supposed to be there.

She searched her desk, her cabinets, behind the blinds on her coveted window, and bile rose in her stomach when she found a tiny black piece of technology attached to the inside of the shade on the standing lamp beside her desk.

She stared down at the small plastic disc in her hand.

Wasn't this all just a little over-the-top?

Okay. Corporate espionage was a thing. She knew that.

And sure, someone could get paid for the information on the Mirrusian royal family, but was it worth all this?

How many devices could there be?

She grabbed her phone and dialed Dima.

"Jenna. Have you had breakfast?" he asked, like everything was normal between them.

"What is it with you and feeding me?" She sighed. "Never mind. Can you have one of your security people come to my office? I found something."

"You are in the office already?"

"Not the issue here."

She was pretty sure he swore in Russian. "I did not expect you to leave the hotel."

"Hmm." She made a noncommittal sound because really? Why hadn't he?

"I thought you would sleep on it and realize that I had your best interests in mind. We should have had breakfast together and then discussed how best to approach what we discovered last night."

"Do you make it a habit of making plans without input from the people they include?"

"I thought we established last night that I do."

"That is not something to be proud of."

"Did I say I was proud of it?"

"Well, if you're not, maybe you should consider changing that habit."

"Perhaps I should. We can talk about it over breakfast."

"I'm already at work."

"You do not need to stay there."

"Yes, I do."

"I will send over the team to do a thorough search of your office while we discuss what they found in your apartment last night."

"We can have that discussion over the phone."

"Please, Jenna, just meet me for breakfast."

"Are you begging me?" she asked with more mockery than she meant to, but the fact that he'd started that sentence with a sincere-sounding *please* was throwing her for a loop. "Why is this so important to you?"

"I'll tell you over breakfast."

"You assume I want to know enough to be swayed by that."

"You may not have the cutthroat nature of some journalists, but you have always had the professional curiosity of one."

"This is hardly a professional situation."

"Agreed, though it impacts your work, as it does mine."

He was right. As much as she hated admitting it. Her situation was impacting his work, and his family.

Though Jenna had not shared any secrets out of turn, sensitive information had leaked through her.

"Fine. Where do you want to meet?"

"I will be at your building in a few minutes to pick you up."

She sighed, not at all surprised that he was already on

the way. If she had refused breakfast, the irritating man would have simply shown up in her office.

Like he had the day before.

"Send your team up. I'll let them in, and then I will come down." She didn't wait for his agreement before hanging up.

Dimitri waited impatiently for Jenna.

He had miscalculated about her leaving the hotel, but that wasn't the only miscalculation he'd made. He'd been so sure that once he told her what was going on, she would understand the need to search her apartment and handbag.

Instead, she'd assumed he'd instigated sex as a maneuver of expediency and was hurt that his family had doubted her at all.

He'd spent more time thinking about her reaction than sleeping the night before and had come to some conclusions. The first was that he should have told her what was going on before having sex with her.

The second was that his brother, Kon, could not seriously have doubted Jenna's innocence. Which raised the question, why had Kon implied that he did?

The passenger door opened, interrupting his thoughts. "We've only got an hour. I called my boss and gave her a heads-up about what is going on. She's meeting me to discuss this situation further when I get back."

Dimitri bit back a curse. "Why did you do that?"

"Because this problem isn't all about you, Your Highness."

Dimitri grimaced. "It never was."

"There's a food truck that has yummy breakfast burritos just around the corner. It's a little chilly, but sunny. We can sit outside and talk."

"A food truck?" he asked, trying to process the very idea. "I can get something delivered."

"To where?" she asked wryly. "The car? Don't be a snob."

Offended, he frowned. "I am not a snob."

"Have you ever eaten from a food truck?"

What difference did that make? "No."

"Then…" Her challenge was clear.

He said he wasn't a snob; prove it.

Grimly determined to do just that, he pulled into traffic, his detail right behind him.

As they walked toward the food truck, Jenna had to admit to herself that eating this way was a different proposition for him than for regular people like her. Jenna had no security detail needing to stay close.

Nor did she have to worry about a random photo shot with a cell phone ending up in the tabloids with some cheesy headline.

Nevertheless, her prince did not grumble as she ordered for them. They got their food and found a nearby bench to sit on.

They'd both taken a couple of bites of their breakfast, washing it down with coffee, when he looked up, his expression tinged with surprise. "This is pretty good."

He looked down at his burrito, like he was trying to figure out what all was in it.

She wished him luck. Jenna had been trying to recreate this particular deliciousness at home for the past two years and had yet to get it just right.

"Don't sound so surprised," she chided him.

"I am not surprised," he denied with dignity. "I am a prince, but I do not live under a rock. Even I know about the food truck craze."

"It's not really a craze anymore, but an established source of dining."

"If you say so."

And he said he wasn't a snob, but Jenna just said, "Tell me what they found in my apartment."

"The listening devices are limited to a few accessory items besides your handbag from last night."

Jenna wasn't sure if she felt relief at that or not. She had a habit of leaving her purse on the end of the sofa, which would have made her living room accessible to the listening device.

All she said was, "Since Skylar's never been to my home, that makes sense."

"Assuming it is your assistant might be premature."

"Like it was premature assuming it was me?" Jenna asked with her brows raised.

Really. These princes. What was okay for them was not okay for the rest of the world.

"I don't think Kon actually ever believed you were the source of the leak." Which made it sound like Dima *never* had, and she doubted that.

Though he'd been clear he didn't doubt her the night before. Jenna crumpled her wrapper and tossed it in a nearby trash can. She set her coffee on the bench beside her and then rubbed her suddenly pounding temples.

"Do you have a headache?"

She rolled her shoulders, the pain receding a bit. "Just a tension one. Are you surprised?"

"No. For what it is worth, Jenna, if I could have spared you knowledge of this, I would have."

"Not what I want to hear." She wasn't some hothouse violet who wanted stuff hidden from her. Not even really hard stuff.

She never had been.

"Why do you say that about Prince Konstantin?" She thought it was pretty obvious he had distrusted her and found it odd that Dima would try to deny it.

"You saw how natural he was with you at dinner. Yes, you two give each other a hard time, but he trusts you with his wife and his children. No way he believes you are a risk to them in any way."

"He came to you." Dima had said so.

"Yes, and I'm still trying to figure out why, but his reasons are not the ones he stated." The prince sounded very certain of his conclusions.

Jenna wasn't convinced. "Oh, I think he wants to know the source of the leaks, all right." Of course he did. Prince Konstantin, like the rest of his family, would never stand for a leak remaining once identified.

"Naturally, but while we both knew it was somehow related to you, I do not believe my brother ever considered you the direct source any more than I did."

"I want to believe that." It would hurt a lot less.

But she wouldn't lie to herself, even if it saved her emotional pain.

"Then believe. I am sure it is the truth." Dima tossed his own trash, his aim as good as hers had been. "If it makes you feel any better, he suggested a lot of ways for me to get the information that weren't dating."

"We didn't date. We had sex."

"Fantastic sex," he clarified, like it was really important. "The dates can come later."

"You think I'm going to date you?" she asked. Again, were they living in the same reality?

"We are not done with each other, Jenna."

"So you say." But she couldn't deny the truth of that statement, so she didn't try to refute it directly.

She still wanted him, even if he was a toad for using sex against her.

At least, that's how it felt.

And it worried her that she was having such an emotional reaction to the timing of them having sex for the first time, because she was feeling things she really, really, really didn't want to.

"Are you going to talk to Emma?" he asked after finishing his coffee.

"And cause an issue with her husband?" Jenna wasn't a monster. Emma and Konstantin had a good marriage, even if the man was a distrustful jerk. "I don't think so. I do have other people to vent to than your royal siblings' wives."

It still rankled they had thought she would have put any stress on Nataliya right now, for any reason.

Dima had the effrontery to look alarmed. "I think even Kon would prefer you kept your venting to Emma."

"Listen, buster, if I want to vent to my own sister, I will. If you don't think she's trustworthy, that's your problem. *She* didn't put a bug in my cell phone stand."

"No, I am sure you are right." They were the right words, but his expression didn't match them fully.

She nodded anyway. He *should* agree with her.

Unfortunately, righteous ire did nothing to diminish her body's response to his nearness. What was it about this man that turned her on so effectively?

He was so not the sort of man she usually dated.

One, he was royal. Two, he was arrogant. Three, he was younger than her. Four, he was a workaholic. Five, he wanted children.

The last caused a twinge in the area of her heart she'd long thought atrophied.

Jenna had stopped grieving what could have been before she'd even let herself start.

"What is the matter?" he asked.

"Nothing. Well, other than the obvious."

"You looked sad for a moment."

She shrugged. "It's nothing."

"If it upsets you, it is not nothing."

"Nice sentiment. Too bad you didn't stick by it last night."

"I should have told you about the possible spy in your life before we had sex." He spoke stiffly, like admitting wrong did not come easily to him.

Only she knew that Dima was better at it than his brothers, at least from what she'd seen. Not that he had much experience admitting mistakes.

He didn't usually make them.

He had last night, though. A big one. And it *had* hurt her. "Yes, you should have."

"I will not make the same call again."

"Good to know." Though how that applied to her, she had no idea, considering the deed was done.

His own nod was decisive. "My security team has had no luck so far tracing the surveillance equipment back to its source."

"I spoke to my boss, and we will be confiscating Skylar's laptop as soon as she arrives in the building." While they'd agreed to meet that morning to discuss how to handle the fallout, that had already been settled during their earlier phone call. "It's the property of the magazine and isn't supposed to have anything private on it, but everyone uses their work laptops for their home stuff too."

Jenna had no doubts that proof of her assistant's spying would be found on that laptop.

If she was wrong, she would apologize, but her instincts

were telling her she wasn't. So many things that in and of themselves had not triggered wariness in Jenna now looked suspect in retrospect.

"Is this true?" he asked. "We have the same policy at Mirrus Global, and I assumed employees followed it."

"Uh…how do I point out that most people don't have the financial means to buy a second computer when they have one supplied from work? There's always something else the money needs to go to."

"You do not have a private system?" he asked, sounding shocked.

"Of course I do. Nataliya is my BFF. Long before she became a princess, then queen, she insisted I have the most up-to-date technology for personal use. I end up using my personal computer for work stuff because it's faster and more secure."

He nodded, like he approved.

Jenna didn't even try not to roll her eyes. "Believe it or not, I'm not really worried what you think of my tech practices."

He laughed. "You are so damn refreshing, Jenna."

"Because I don't care what you think?"

"I'm not sure that is entirely true, but yes. Because you are not and have never been in awe of my family."

"You're the family of my BFF. If I was in awe of you, it would be awkward for her and me." And Jenna wasn't letting any awkwardness get between her and Nataliya.

"You two are very close."

"And you thought I would go crying to her if you asked me about the leak." Jenna let her disgust at that reasoning shade her voice. "You and Prince Konstantin need to take a course in reading people, because you sure showed some illiteracy when it came to me."

"You are right, and for that I apologize."

"You apologize for that, but not for using sex against me?"

"I did say I was sorry for hurting you," he pointed out. "I have acknowledged I should have apprised you of the situation before we had sex. However, I will not lie and say I am sorry we had sex."

"You're honest, at least." If he'd been honest about his motives for the sex, she wouldn't be so hurt now.

His timing had been so wrong, and him acknowledging it didn't make it all better.

"I was honest last night too," he said, like he was reading her mind. "I wanted you. The fact that we had to search your apartment and your things didn't influence that."

"But if you'd told me about it before…" She let her voice trail off on a sigh.

He knew he was wrong. She needed to leave it at that.

"You might have been so focused on the leak, you would have said no to the sex."

Shocked, Jenna almost dropped what remained of her coffee. "That is quite an admission."

"That I wanted you so badly I was willing to compromise my own integrity in order to have you?" He did not sound happy. "And am just now realizing it? It is not my finest moment."

Okay, that right there made her feel better. He was too genuinely upset to be shining her on about this.

And for a guy who prided himself on his integrity, recognizing he'd compromised it wouldn't be easy. That could explain why he'd been so dense about it the night before.

"I accept your apology, but if it has something to do with me, you cannot hide it from me. You understand that now, right?"

"That is not how I usually operate. Filtering information is something I was taught from an early age."

"Like the whole don't show emotion thing?" Which he didn't seem to be so successful at with her.

"Yes."

"You can unlearn anything you have been taught."

"I am not sure that is true."

"Try it and see."

He put his hand out for her empty coffee cup and then tossed it. "I am not going to start being a fount of information or transparency."

"No doubt, but if it has to do with me, then you tell me. That's not hard."

He looked like he would argue.

She put up her hand, silencing him without words. "Listen, Dima, if you want me to trust you, you have to trust me."

"I do trust you." He grabbed her hand and then brought it to his mouth to kiss the backs of her fingers, his expression all about sexual intent and not at all about promising full disclosure. "We have established this."

In his mind, maybe.

"Fine," she conceded. "If you trust me, then you don't withhold information from me that relates to me. I'm not asking for state secrets here."

He stood up and drew her with him, heading back toward the cars. "Maybe."

"What do you mean, maybe?" That connection between them, her hand in his, was doing weird things to her.

Not just sexual things, either, and that had her biting her lip with worry.

"It could relate to you and still be a state secret," he explained.

"For crying out loud," she said with exasperation. "You do not need to conjure up every potential scenario. What are the chances of that, really?"

Color burnished his cheeks.

Oh, wow, he was embarrassed.

"It is my nature to look at all potential outcomes." He sounded almost humble.

"Or you were taught that too."

"Regardless, it is far too ingrained."

"I believe you, but maybe just accept that not all of them are going to come to pass and let them go."

"That is not my way."

"I know Nikolai is the oldest, and the king, but seriously, Dima, I swear you outdo him."

"What do you mean?"

"Well, I think you may be more arrogantly certain of your own ideas than even he is."

"My brother listens to counsel."

"While you keep your own."

Dima didn't say anything, possibly realizing the attempt to refute her words would force him to lie.

"You're also more of a worrier."

"I do not worry."

"What would you call going through every possible doomsday scenario before you commit to a course of action?"

"Being responsible."

That surprised a laugh out of her. "Promise me anyway, Dima."

"I like when you use my name."

He'd said so, and maybe her use of his title had been as much to annoy him as establish emotional distance when she was so hurt and angry.

"Great. I'll make a deal with you. As long as you exhibit trust in me that is in line with being my friend—"

"And lover," he slotted in, interrupting her like he never interrupted anyone.

"That's still up for debate." Though she hadn't pulled her hand from his, had she? "Anyway, as long as you do that, then I will call you Dima."

"This includes telling you about things like the leak of confidential information that coincided with your visits and video calls with Nataliya?"

She'd thought they'd already established that, but she gave him verbal agreement anyway. "Yes."

He thought for several long seconds.

Jenna's tension grew with each one, and she realized this was way more important to her than it should be. She didn't even try and lie to herself that it was all about her relationship with Nataliya and her BFF's family. This was about Jenna and Dima, about him *being* Dima to her and not Prince Dimitri, like his brother would always be Prince Konstantin.

"I agree," he said solemnly.

Air whooshed out of her in relief, but she still went for casual with her tone. "Good."

CHAPTER SEVEN

THE NEXT FEW hours were more than a little stressful.

It turned out that Skylar had a lot more than just a link to audio files in the cloud from her listening devices that was incriminating on her laptop.

She had pictures of designs that Jenna had kept in a locked filing cabinet in her office, and information files about Mirrus Global and even Jenna's brother's company.

However, because neither the royal family nor Jenna's boss wanted the negative publicity it would bring, both were adamant about not pressing charges.

The magazine actually had a policy to the effect that if an employee was found doing this sort of thing, they were to be fired, but that was all.

Jenna was furious. "It was my privacy that was violated, and yours are not the only companies affected by her criminality."

Skylar just stood there looking smug. Like she knew she could be fired but wasn't facing anything worse.

"Let us be clear," Dima said coldly to Skylar. "If a single piece of sensitive information about my family or company gets leaked from this point, we will not only press charges here in the US, but we will charge you with espionage and file for extradition."

Skylar paled at this but did not reply. When the magazine's editorial director made a similar, if less impressive, threat in regard to information related to the magazine, the editorial assistant didn't even blink.

"They might be content not to file charges against you, but I'm not," Jenna informed the other woman, her fury renewed by Skylar's smug attitude. "And considering the information you had stored in regard to my brother's company, I doubt he will be either."

Both Dima and Jenna's boss went tense at Jenna's words. She did not care. Yes, she understood that it could be damaging for the matter to go public, but this woman had spied on her and other people through her.

What was to stop Skylar from doing the same thing again, if there were no consequences?

"Jenna, surely you understand that would not be the best circumstance for the magazine?" her boss pointed out, her tone not nearly as autocratic as usual.

Because she had to realize it was Jenna's choice and not hers. She also must see the willingness in Jenna to deal with the fallout for going against company policy. Who had a policy about stuff like this?

Her magazine that she was just thinking that morning was so much better than other media companies, that's who.

"You and His Highness are acting like you are the only ones affected, and you are not." He wasn't Dima when he was trying to get Jenna to back down on something so important to her. He couldn't be.

A true friend would not ask her to sweep being stalked and spied on under the carpet like it had never happened.

"A promising new designer lost her company and her reputation because of this woman. *I* thought she was being ridiculous accusing me of selling her designs. You did that, and you knew what you were doing when you did."

Skylar looked almost bored. "New designers fail every day."

Jenna gasped at that cold response. "She didn't have to. She could have made it." Jenna had been certain she would. It was why she'd planned an entire spread on the designer's spring collection.

Dismissing the woman who clearly had no conscience, Jenna spoke to her boss. "I don't know what Skylar has passed on about my brother's company, but I aim to find out."

"What are you going to do, have me arrested for listening to you talk to your brother on the phone?" Skylar sneered now.

"Yes, that exactly." Jenna let her livid glare settle on Skylar again. "This state has stalking laws, and I'm pretty sure you've violated most of them."

That brought a look of consternation to her *former* assistant's face, but then she rallied. "I didn't harass you. That's not stalking. Regardless, the magazine has too much to lose to let you do that."

"Here's the thing you don't seem to get. It is not up to them. You spied on *me*, not the magazine." And if it wasn't stalking, it still wasn't legal. Jenna was sure of that.

"Jenna," Dima said in a flat tone.

She turned to him. "What?"

"Can we speak privately for a moment?"

"I don't know. It doesn't look like any of my conversations have been private for the past year or more."

Dima's head of security stepped forward. "Your office is clean."

Genuine gratitude washed over her at that knowledge, and she let it show in her eyes. "Thank you."

Dima gave his security guy a look and then indicated the direction of her office with his hand. "Shall we?"

Jenna nodded before leading him from the room.

They got to her office, and he shut the door behind them, then turned to face her, his expression bordering on sympathetic. "You know you cannot press charges."

"Um…no, I *do not* know that."

"What kind of stress do you think Nataliya will feel to find out that someone has been spying on you for a year?"

She couldn't believe he was playing the BFF health guilt card with her. "Don't tell her."

"You really expect her not to find out?"

He might not believe it, no matter what he'd said earlier, but no way would Jenna even consider going through with pressing charges if she thought it could lead to unhealthy stress for her friend. "You and your brothers are resourceful. I'm sure you can keep the news from her."

"Like anyone has ever been able to keep a secret from her. She's a hacker."

And a darn good one, but Nataliya was too busy with her roles as queen, wife, and mom to indulge in her love for digging out secrets unless she needed to.

"If she was monitoring me that closely, she would already know, and she would have been the one to come to me. She only researches what she needs to know, and right now she's focused on a whole lot besides the nitty-gritty of her BFF's life."

"Without the threat of prosecution, that woman is not going to keep silent about any of this," Dima said, taking another tack. "For all we know, she is already aware of Nataliya's pregnancy, and it is not supposed to be made public for another month."

"How well do you know your sister-in-law?" Jenna asked Dima, her tone dry.

"I would say very well."

"Then you know that if it were left up to her, Nataliya

would want Skylar prosecuted to the very extent of the law in order to protect others from being harmed. Besides, you can still threaten her with extradition and longer prison time."

"A conviction isn't going to stop a woman like her from doing this again," Dima said cynically. "She's found a way to augment her income, and she's not giving it up just because she goes to jail for a while."

"So I'll sue her in civil court and bankrupt her. Besides, a conviction *will* make it a heck of a lot harder for Skylar to get a job where she has access to sensitive information. If I'd known she had a sideline selling information, I wouldn't have let her near me or my work."

Jenna couldn't help feeling responsible for hiring the woman regardless. She'd *liked* Skylar and had planned to mentor her career as Jenna had been mentored back in the day.

Dima gave her a grim look. "Jenna, do you remember the NDA you signed after Nataliya and my brother became engaged?"

Where was he going with this? "Of course."

"It prevents you from pressing charges against Skylar, because to do so would require you to reveal sensitive information about my family and company."

"I don't have to reveal that she stole information about you all and Mirrus Global." She would be perfectly happy to keep that out of either a criminal or civil suit.

"Any investigation would do so in its natural course, and that would put you in breach of the agreement."

"I'm not sure a lawyer would agree."

"By all means, consult with one." He didn't sound superior but resigned.

And Jenna knew then that Dima was certain of his legal standing. Additionally, he was willing to use her own integrity against her, if it meant getting what he wanted. She'd signed that NDA in good faith, more than willing to promise to keep her friend's secrets.

"So my brother and his company don't matter?" Jenna asked, disillusioned in a way she had never been before.

Not even last night, when she'd thought he'd used sex as nothing more than a tool.

"We will determine if any harm has been done to his company and what can be done to mitigate it." Dima said that like his promise was worth anything to her, and moreover that such a promise should be enough.

But how could she trust him to care about her brother's company? Or her brother, for that matter, when it was so obvious he didn't care about Jenna?

Jenna wanted to call Nataliya more than anything in that moment.

And knew it really was the last thing she *could* do.

"Fine." Jenna had no other words.

Her own sense of honor wouldn't let her go forward with plans that might mean the world to her, but also violated a promise she'd made. Even if she hadn't understood that promise to include a situation like this when she'd made it.

"Fine? Does that mean we are in agreement, then?" he asked.

"If you mean, do we agree that you have my hands tied? Yes."

His jaw tautened, but he nodded. "Pressing charges would not have the all-encompassing benefit you seem to think."

"Justice is not just a benefit." It was something you either believed in, or you didn't.

He obviously didn't believe Jenna deserved it, or that the woman who had done her harm deserved to be served with it.

Dima frowned, but after a quick look at his watch, opened the door. "Shall we?"

"No."

That stopped him. "You agreed."

"You don't need me in there to tell Skylar that she's won and can go on to do exactly what she's done to me to someone else."

"That is not what is going to happen."

But Jenna wasn't listening. "Close the door on your way out."

"Jenna—"

"We're finished here. Now get out of my office, Your Highness."

"I understand that you are upset—"

"Save it," she interrupted again, absolutely done with this conversation.

The look on his face would have been funny if her heart wasn't so sore. How had she left herself open to him and his family hurting her? Again?

Twice in twenty-four hours. Ignoring that would make her beyond foolish.

Being friends with a queen had its ups and downs, but for the first time, Jenna questioned whether staying in Nataliya's life was worth it.

Instead of listening to her, Dima stepped back toward Jenna, like he was ready to talk this out.

Only she'd given him that kind of chance once already, and hours later he was betraying her again.

"No." She shook her head, emphasizing her refusal to go there. "You have not only just told me that can I not seek justice for a terrible violation of my trust and privacy, but you have informed me that I cannot even tell my brother or other family about it. Not for his sake, not for mine."

"We can arrange for a palace-approved therapist for you

to talk to," Dima said, sounding like he really thought that was some kind of solution.

"How about you arrange a way to tell my best friend that I can't be in her life anymore?"

"No, that's not—"

"Your choice." She glared at Dima, Jenna's eyes burning with tears, her heart cracking at the thought of losing Nataliya. "I won't put other people in my life at risk because I want to keep a dear person in my life."

"You don't mean that."

"Honestly? I don't know, but right now, I do know I don't want you in my office. Can you respect that, at least, Your Highness?"

"Jenna, I respect you."

The look she gave him let him know how much she believed that.

His frown of consternation said he got the message. "Your boss is just as committed to not pressing charges."

Like that mattered. It wasn't her boss in here pressing the advantage and giving Jenna a gag order.

"I didn't have sex with my boss last night. She's never claimed I was part of her family." She spoked slowly, so he did not miss a single word. "She didn't pretend to be my friend."

"It is no pretense. Do you think I would press charges if it had been me who was being spied on?" he asked. "Or one of my brothers?"

"Does it matter? It wasn't you. It was me, and I want Skylar to go to jail."

"You're not a vengeful person."

Justice was not vengeance, but if he couldn't see that, Jenna saying so wasn't going to open his eyes.

A knock sounded at the door.

Jenna made no move to answer it. Doing so would require her walking right by Dima, and she wasn't doing that.

After a second knock, the prince turned around and opened the door. His security guy said something in a low tone.

Dima nodded and replied in the same quiet tone, then turned back to her. "I have to leave."

Since that was what she'd been trying to get him to do for the last several minutes, Jenna did not bother to reply.

"There's a problem with the deal I'm working for Mirrus Global," he offered anyway.

"Okay."

"Can I pick you up for dinner?"

She didn't even ask herself what planet he lived on. He'd established it wasn't in her orbit. "No."

"Jenna, we have to talk."

"No."

"Yes." Then he left.

Jenna took a deep breath and then let it out. Everything just felt too heavy to hold right now.

So she did what she always did when emotion got too heavy. She focused on something else.

Back when her brother had been dying, she'd gotten straight A's and been named player of the year on her soccer team.

Right now, she had a magazine to get out.

Moving to her desk, she powered up her laptop and got to work.

The next couple of days, Jenna ignored several calls and texts from Dima.

She hid her feelings from Nataliya, but that was easy via text. They had a video call scheduled on the weekend, and Jenna was seriously considering coming up with an excuse to get out of it.

Even if she had to lie.

Jenna and her boss had spoken briefly about the situation, and while the older woman had been sorry for how violated Jenna must feel, she'd been adamant that the magazine's reputation would suffer terrible harm if it got out that they'd had such a serious and long-lasting breach in their confidentiality.

No one seemed to care about the designer who had lost her business over that breach, or what potential harm could come to Jenna's brother's company, or how many other people had been harmed by Skylar's information leaks.

Not to mention, the woman had profited by her perfidy and had gotten away with it.

Sure, she'd been fired, but the carefully worded reason for doing so had left it possible for her to file for unemployment benefits even.

Jenna was beyond livid, and that feeling wasn't going away.

Her relationship with Nataliya wasn't the only thing she was reevaluating in her life. She didn't know if she wanted to continue working for the magazine.

She was also hurt. Her life and privacy had been invaded, and that was going to go unanswered.

She couldn't even talk about it to her two dearest friends, much less her family, and that inability was making everything feel bigger and more ugly.

And under all of it was this pain in her heart that centered around Dima.

Something she didn't even want to acknowledge, because the sex was supposed to be just that and not emotionally driven. Only she felt deep and pain-filled emotion every time his name flashed on her phone screen.

Thankfully, he hadn't shown up unannounced to her work again.

Jenna didn't know what she was going to do about her friendship with Nataliya and Emma.

She'd never thought the cost for having them in her life would be so high, that her personal integrity would be compromised.

She felt guilty about the people whose secrets had been betrayed because of her and wanted to tell them it had happened.

The fact that she couldn't only added to the maelstrom of negative emotion swirling constantly inside her.

While she had no intention of going to a palace-approved therapist, Jenna thought finding a local one to talk to might not be a bad idea. She didn't want to keep feeling this way.

And she needed to talk to someone. Jenna loved Nataliya like a sister, but she cared deeply for Emma too, and both their children were like nieces and nephews to Jenna.

Only how could she stay in their life if it meant she had to lie? To hide damaging truths?

And yet, how could Jenna leave their lives without causing Nataliya stress that would be dangerous to her and her unborn child right now?

Her phone rang, the ringtone her brother's, and guilt washed over her anew.

While she was perfectly happy to avoid Dima's calls, Jenna wasn't a coward, and she wasn't going to do the same for Luke. She swiped to answer. "Hey, little brother."

"I just got off the phone with Prince Dimitri."

"Oh?" she asked, wondering why Dima would have called Luke.

Had he been checking to make sure she hadn't spilled the truth to Luke?

"What the hell, Jenna? You had someone spying on you

for over a year! Are you okay?" Her brother's tone left no doubt how worried about her he was.

It was like a balm to Jenna's soul.

"He told you that?" Jenna could barely believe it.

Why would Dima do that?

"He made me do an electronic signature on an NDA first, but yes. That guy is a year younger than me, but I don't mind admitting he intimidates me."

Jenna surprised herself with a laugh. She hadn't felt much like laughing the last few days. "He's a prince. It's in the job description."

"You think? I never got the impression anyone in that family intimidated you."

"They don't."

"Then why didn't you tell us what happened?"

Jenna grimaced. "I signed an NDA too, a long time ago. Telling you would have breached it."

"Like any of us would have let them know," her brother scoffed.

"My integrity was already ripped to shreds. I wasn't flushing it down the sewer too."

Her brother's sigh was long. "Jenna, you expect too much from yourself. You didn't do anything wrong."

"I hired the wrong person. I made friends with the wrong person."

"What the hell are you talking about?"

"Nataliya. Being friends with her painted a target on your back, and I didn't even know it."

"There is no target on my back. Has anyone ever told you that you take your role as the oldest way too seriously?"

"I'm not the oldest." Matt had died, but he'd lived too, and she'd never claim his spot in their family.

"No, I know." This sigh was a lot less gusty.

Luke understood how important that distinction was.

She was the oldest surviving sibling, but she would never actually be the oldest.

"Listen, sis, you need to stop taking yourself so seriously. You weren't the only one who approved your assistant. In fact, I doubt she was hired right into her position."

"She wasn't." Oh, man, had they bothered to look into the two years Skylar had worked at the magazine before she'd become Jenna's assistant?

"Right," he said, like he'd had no doubt. "Skylar is an opportunist. She wasn't just selling information about the royal family, but about designers—"

"And your company. She had a file on it." That still bothered Jenna. A lot.

"Sure, but nothing really actionable to work with. You are about as interested in genetic research as I am in fashion. We don't talk business."

That was true. "But she had a file."

"A useless one with no information that isn't already public. Prince Dimitri made sure I got a copy so I could mitigate any potential damage. Stop feeling guilty about me and my company. We are both fine."

"Did Dima tell you to call me?" Jenna asked.

"Yes. He thought you needed someone to talk to because you aren't talking to any of them."

Okay, so she'd neglected to return Emma's latest phone call and her text trying to firm up plans for dinner again.

"I don't want to talk to them."

"Why? You're closer to Nataliya than Lisa," he said, mentioning their youngest sister.

"Lisa and I are close."

"I didn't say you weren't, just that you're closer to your BFF."

Jenna sighed. "I can't talk to her about this. She needs stress minimized in her life right now."

"Is she pregnant again?" her brother asked, no slouch in the thinking department.

"Yes."

"So why not Emma then?"

"I just don't know if being friends with their family is worth it."

"Worth what exactly?"

"Being forced to lie."

"About what?"

"This. All of it. I couldn't tell you that your privacy had been breached, and you're my brother!"

"So, Prince Dimitri made it so you could."

"He probably expects me to be grateful."

"Probably. He strikes me as the kind of man who thinks he knows what's best for everyone else."

"You wouldn't know anything about that, would you?"

Her brother laughed, but they both knew that described him too.

"Maybe you should take some time off."

"You think that will help?" she asked, not against the idea, just not convinced it would make any difference.

"You're a dweller, Jenna. You've had to come into that office where that opportunistic piece of work planted a listening device every day since you found out. Tell me you don't wonder if someone is listening in on your calls, if somehow somebody hasn't breached the security on that laptop Nataliya tricked out for you."

"I can honestly say that particular worry is a nonstarter."

"And the other."

"I hate being in my office. Hate it. And it's an exercise in willpower answering the phone. Every single time."

"Is that why you're ignoring Prince Dimitri's calls?"

"He told you that?"

"Sure. Everybody knows you two have feelings for each

other. Just because you've never acted on them doesn't negate their existence."

Jenna gasped and flailed before sputtering out, "Lust is not a feeling."

"Sure it is, but I'm not talking about lust, and you know it."

"Who is everybody?" she demanded, rather than react to that bit of provocation.

"The family. And if our family sees it, I'm sure his does too."

"You all are delusional."

"The only one here not seeing reality is you, if you think the way you two feel about each other isn't obvious to the people who know you best."

"I would prefer my baby brother not speculate on my sex life."

He made a gagging sound. "Definitely not doing that."

"It can't be any more than that."

"It already is."

"It can't be," she emphasized. "And you know why."

Her brother was silent long enough she hoped he had dropped it.

"He's the youngest, not the oldest," Luke pointed out, though. "He doesn't have to have children for primogeniture."

"Ooh, big words."

"I use big words all the time. I run a genetic research lab."

More like a group of labs, but why quibble over terminology?

"Listen, brother mine, even if there was a chance that Dima and I could have ever had something…" And she was convinced there was not. "There isn't one now. I can't trust him."

"Because he made you stay silent about what happened?"

"That's part of it." A big part of it.

"But here we are, talking about it because he made that possible."

"Stop. You probably think that's awesome of him, but you aren't the only one Skylar had a file on. I can't go to any of those other companies or designers and warn them."

"You'd get fired if you did."

"Maybe."

"Would it be worth it?"

"Maybe."

"Jenna, sometimes we have to do the hard thing because one set of priorities trumps another."

"His will always be his family. You think I want even a casual relationship with someone who will throw me under the bus so easily?"

"He didn't."

"That's how it feels."

"Again, take some time. You need to figure out what is reality and what is feeling."

Luke had a point. Though she could argue that feelings were as real as anything else in life. Only she knew Luke didn't share that viewpoint.

He was a scientist and a businessman.

He and Dima probably had more in common in how they thought than Jenna and the prince did.

Still, she felt the need to elaborate. "The fact Dima doesn't understand how important it is to me that Skylar be arrested for her crimes, that she be prevented from waltzing into another company and doing the exact same thing, shows how far apart our priorities are."

The royal family weren't the only ones who mattered. Not even Nataliya.

That's not the way the world became a better place, and Jenna believed in change.

She didn't mention the whole "sex to get her out of her apartment so it could be searched" thing. Jenna accepted that Dima really hadn't seen the sex as a convenient diversion, but something inevitable between them.

She could not deny that inevitability with any level of honesty either.

"You don't know what measures the prince has taken to protect the other people your assistant spied on through you. Maybe give him a chance to tell you before you write him off completely."

"I told you—"

"That you have no future because you can't have children."

She sucked in air, the truth something she hadn't needed to say out loud since her decision at the age of twenty-one to make sure the genetic disease that killed her brother could not be passed on through her.

When she and her two younger siblings had been tested for the gene, only she had been a carrier. For Jenna, no other decision could be made but to have a tubal ligation and prevent any chance of her passing the gene on to the next generation.

Luke cursed. "I didn't say that to hurt you."

"I know." She wished she could say it didn't hurt, but the wound she'd thought healed long ago felt fresh and new.

"My point is, it's not the roadblock to a future with Prince Dimitri you think it is."

"I know you believe that."

"But you don't."

"This is a nonsensical discussion. You do realize that, don't you?"

Luke let her change the subject, but Jenna kept thinking about her brother's suggestion that she take time off over the following week.

CHAPTER EIGHT

With each day, it grew harder for Jenna to go into her office, and the idea of taking time off became more appealing.

A last-minute emergency at work made it possible for her to avoid her video chat with Nataliya, but Jenna knew she couldn't avoid her BFF for long, and she needed to make some hard decisions about her relationship with the royal family.

Either she sucked it up and dealt with the compromises she had to make, or she walked away.

Her current level of exhaustion wasn't helping her apply rational thinking to it either. Jenna had had trouble sleeping ever since discovering she had been spied on. She would wake up in a cold sweat convinced she was being watched, only to have to convince herself it wasn't true before going back to sleep.

If she could go back to sleep.

Even though all her clothes and accessories had been cleared, she'd been dressing without her usual styling as well. She hadn't carried a purse since the night she'd made love with Dima.

She'd gone out and bought a new laptop bag, but for some reason couldn't make herself use a purse at all.

The job she had always loved was now a source of irri-

tation and frustration. Jenna didn't want to return emails
or calls from designers wanting to give her an early peek
at their new collections.

Jenna wasn't just avoiding Emma's calls. She still found
answering the phone nearly impossible.

No question, she needed a change of pace.

It started with asking for time off. If she came back
with the intention of staying at the magazine, she would
request a change of office locations. She would give up
her window to get away from the sense of violation she
felt every time she walked into her office.

Her boss approved the leave without a single argument,
and Jenna went home, not sure if she was going to take a
trip or just putter around her apartment for the next two
weeks.

Her phone rang as she was walking in her door. Jenna
grabbed it from her jacket pocket, where she'd been keeping it, and glanced at the caller ID.

Dima.

She swiped to answer. All sorts of snarky greetings
went through her mind, but Jenna was a grown-up, so she
went with, "Hello?"

"Jenna. You answered." He sounded shocked.

"Didn't you want me to?"

"I would not have called you otherwise."

"Okay."

"You talked to your brother."

"I did."

"Did it help?"

"With my feelings of guilt or betrayal?"

"Either?"

"Both actually." Though she also planned to take Luke's
advice about asking Dima what he'd done to protect other

people's information compromised by Skylar, since they couldn't be told about the leak.

"Then I am glad you spoke to him."

"That's not what you were saying in my office."

"I may have been overzealous in telling you not to speak to your family."

"Really? Because I reread that NDA your father had me sign, and it was pretty airtight. There were no exceptions."

"Yes, well, your family isn't going to blab to the press."

"No, they are not, but you still had my brother sign an NDA before you told him what happened."

"I'm a cautious guy."

"Is that part of being a prince too?"

"I wish you didn't say the word *prince* with such loathing," he said, his own tone almost wistful. "I am certain that caution is part of my nature and has little to do with my position as prince."

"You could be right," she acceded.

"I have to fly back to New York."

"You have been in Seattle all this time?" she asked, surprised as she dropped her wallet and other things she'd been carrying in her pockets in a small pile in the center of her table.

"No, I flew to Mirrus for a few days to meet with Nikolai and Konstantin."

"Emma texted that Konstantin was out of town."

Jenna had replied to her friend's texts but still avoided committing to getting together in person.

"He wants to apologize for allowing you to think he doubted your loyalty to Nataliya."

"Implying he didn't doubt it?" she asked with skepticism.

"I told you that he didn't."

"And yet you are also the one who told me he did."

"He did say so," Dima said, sounding a tad defensive. "When I confronted him about it, he admitted he'd never doubted you."

"Then why did he say he did?" she asked, still irked and, yes, hurt by it.

She'd cared about this family for a good part of a decade. Believing that some of them had not trusted her had been painful.

"He never really gave a straight answer, just that we'd needed the leak shored up, and he'd known I was the one to make that happen."

"Well, he was right," she acknowledged.

"You were hurt in the process."

"Yes." Why deny a truth they both knew?

"I am sorry."

She bit back a sigh. "I believe you."

"Because I called your brother?"

"Well, that and the fact you keep calling. You could have just let things go, but you didn't."

"You were thinking about giving up our family."

She had said she was considering ending her friendship with Nataliya. It was funny he put it that way, as if Jenna was walking away from all of them.

Which she would be, but still. Nataliya was her BFF. Jenna hadn't really thought the rest of the family saw her as part of *their* lives as well, despite claiming she was family.

People said stuff like that without meaning it all the time.

"I'm still thinking about it."

He said something under his breath.

"What did you say?" she asked.

"It is not important." His tone said otherwise. "I wanted to see you before I go back to New York."

"I'm not sure that's a good idea." Jenna needed a clear

head to think about her future, and being around Dima clouded her mind and heart.

With lust, yes, but also with feelings she knew could go nowhere.

There was no win in that scenario for her.

Well, unless she considered mind-blowing orgasms a win. And in this case, she wasn't sure they wouldn't contribute to the problem.

"It is a good idea," he assured her with certainty ringing in his voice. "Me leaving town again without seeing you is not."

Knowing he couldn't see it, but unable to stop herself, Jenna shook her head in negation. She opened her mouth to say the denial out loud when her eyes flicked over a bunch of travel brochures she'd picked up in the middle of winter.

Dreaming about visiting sunny beaches had lifted her spirits when the skies were overcast and the never-ending rain of winter kept coming down in sheets so that even taking a walk was a challenge.

She loved Seattle, but sometimes when it rained nonstop for a week or more, she thought about what it would be like to *live* somewhere sunny. Not just visit.

"Unfortunately, I need to pack." Because she was going to pick one of those sunny destinations and go.

Wherever she could book for flight and accommodations starting tomorrow. Jenna wasn't picky. She just wanted to get away.

"Pack for what?"

"I'm going on vacation."

"Where?"

"Not sure yet, but someplace sunny."

"You don't know where you are going?" he asked like the idea was beyond comprehension.

"No."

"But you are leaving tomorrow?" The disbelief in his voice came across loud and clear over their connection.

"Yes."

He was silent for a full five seconds. "Is that a good idea?" he asked, almost tentatively.

Imagine, Prince Dimitri of the House of Merikov tentative.

"Why wouldn't it be?"

"Perhaps you are reacting to what happened." He said the words slowly and carefully, like they were nitroglycerin he didn't want to detonate.

"I'm definitely reacting to it." And she had no trouble admitting that. "I want to get away, to enjoy some stress-free days on a beach somewhere."

And to think through what she should do going into the future, away from everything familiar.

"And you do not know where?" He was sounding almost panicked.

"Why does that bother you so much? Normal people go on spur-of-the-moment vacations all the time. That's why there's last-minute deals, for people like me."

She started sifting through the brochures and stopped at the one for Abu Dhabi. As funny as it might sound, she'd always wanted to go, ever since reading the *Garfield* comics as a child. The big orange cat was always threatening to ship Opie there.

As an adult, she'd learned it was the capital of the UAE, and that had only made it seem more intriguing and a place she wanted to go.

Jenna loved traveling, but her trips were usually dictated by work. This time, she was going on vacation, and she could go anywhere she liked.

"I've got to go, Dima. I need to get my trip booked."

After a quick search, she'd discovered she didn't need

a visa to travel the UAE as long as her passport was current, which it was.

"You aren't seriously booking a trip today that you plan to leave on tomorrow?" There was that odd near-panicked tone in the princely voice again.

"Well, yes." Or perhaps the next day, but she was really hoping for tomorrow.

"What if it is a scam?"

"I'm not booking on some random website. I'll use my usual links. You really need to get over this travel paranoia."

"I am not paranoid about travel," he said with stiff dignity.

"I'm glad to hear it. I was getting worried."

He made a strange sound, like he was choking, trying to talk and growling at the same time.

She laughed. She kind of liked eliciting that sound from the urbane prince.

"Where are you hoping to go?" he asked.

"I told you, I don't know. Someplace sunny." She didn't mention Abu Dhabi because that probably would sound like pie in the sky, and she realized her chances of booking anything for there in the immediate future were slim.

"Surely you have a destination you are hoping for?"

"I didn't," she said grudgingly.

"But now you do?"

"Abu Dhabi. I know I'll probably end up in Mexico." Last-minute bookings for cruises to Mexico and all-inclusive resorts were always being offered in the ads on the sidebars of her favorite travel sites. "But I'm going to look anyway."

"Do not let me keep you, then."

Jenna hung up, ignoring the disappointment she felt to

be saying goodbye to the man she knew was not good for her. He'd hurt her, more than once.

Maintaining their friendship, much less pursuing something sexual with him, was not a good idea.

And yet, she didn't like that he'd given up so easily on the idea of seeing her before he left Seattle.

An hour later, Jenna was staring morosely at her computer. Not only were there no last-minute trips to Abu Dhabi she could get in on, but she'd realized that she didn't want to settle, and that left her not booking anything at all.

Dispirited, she got up to make herself a cup of tea when her doorbell rang.

Not expecting anyone, she checked the peephole in her door. Dima stood on the other side, his expression expectant.

She should be irritated, and she was, but she also felt pleasure at the sight of him. A small voice in the back of her mind rejoiced that he had refused to leave town without seeing her.

Even after everything.

And that was seriously scary.

She could not afford to catch deep feelings for a man she simply could *not* make a future with.

She opened the door to her small single-level ranch-style home. Her brother had suggested a condo in a secure building, but Jenna had wanted her own space, and she'd never regretted her decision to buy a single-dwelling house instead.

She pulled open the door. "Dima, what are you doing here?"

"Bringing you dinner." He held up a bag of takeaway from one of her favorite restaurants.

She had a choice. Jenna could refuse him entrance,

or she could let him in. If she let him in, she was tacitly agreeing to talk to him.

That did not mean she was agreeing to continuing their sexual relationship, she reminded herself. And she had not yet asked him if he had done anything to protect others from Skylar's willingness to sell secrets to the highest bidder.

"Come in." She stepped back to let him inside.

One of his security guys came first, taking *the tour*, as she thought of it before declaring the house clear. He left, pulling the door shut behind them.

"Won't he be conspicuous standing on my stoop?" she asked.

"My security does not stand on stoops. They will take up noninvasive positions that allow them to watch your house from all approachable angles."

"Do you ever get tired of all of that?" she asked, leading the way into the L-shaped living and dining area.

He set the takeout bag on the dining table. "Security, you mean?"

"Yes. You can't ever just run down to the corner store and buy a candy bar."

"I've mostly always had them." There was a shrug in his voice even if he was too controlled to follow through with his shoulders. "I've never once *wanted* to run down to the corner store for anything. And as we discussed before, it's as much about my wealth as my royal lineage."

Jenna shook her head, and swept the brochures into a pile and removed them from her dining table, where she'd had them spread out in hopeful array. "I would hate living like that."

"You would be surprised what you can become accustomed to." The look he gave her said there was more than the surface message in those words.

Though she had no clue what it was meant to be.

"Maybe," she said noncommittally as she pulled out plates and cutlery. "What if I'd already eaten?"

"Have you?"

"No."

"Then the point is moot."

"I suppose. I'm sure I told you I would be busy packing."

"You need to eat."

Her stomach chose that moment to growl, and she didn't even bother trying to deny it. "I'll plate up."

It took only a minute or so to do just that, and then she cleared away the detritus of the takeaway, something she'd always done when eating takeout at home.

She liked sitting at the table and eating off plates, using real forks.

He settled in one of her dining chairs, and the table that was large enough to accommodate her family for holiday dinners suddenly felt intimate. "Have you booked your vacation yet?"

"No." She took a bite of her pasta, savoring it and realizing at once how hungry she'd gotten. "There are tons of trips I could take to Southern Cali, or Mexico."

"But nothing for Abu Dhabi?"

"Nothing." Well, not nothing, but no trips in her price range.

He gave her a warm look. "Perhaps I can help."

"Have you taken up travel bookings in all that spare time you don't have?" she asked while doing her best to pretend her entire body wasn't responding to that look.

"Not personally, but I have staff."

"And you asked them to look into a trip for me?" she asked, surprised.

"For *us*."

Warning bells started clanging in her head. "What do you mean?"

"A tsunami of bad timing hit us last week, but we were far from done with each other, *milaya*."

He was talking about sex. Jenna's body gave a big *whomp* of response to the thought. "I thought you were in the middle of a huge deal."

"We finalized it last week when I was in Mirrus. It will make the company millions and provide additional infra-structure on Mirrus."

"That's amazing." It couldn't be easy to provide local jobs for an island country that limited tourism.

"Thank you. I thought so. My brothers were both pleased, as well."

And that would be important to a man who was every bit as alpha as either of his older brothers but would always be the youngest sibling.

"I deserve to celebrate," Dima proclaimed.

"You seem like the kind of man who celebrates one good deal by starting another one, not going on a trip with your current casual sexual partner."

"Usually you would be right, but you see, this woman I cannot get out of my system, she wants to go on a va-cation."

"That's a pretty big admission."

"You led me to believe last-minute vacations are quite normal for people."

"People who aren't royalty, yes, or, you know…workaholic tycoons, but that's not what I meant."

"Oh?"

"Stop playing naive," she instructed him with just a tinge of annoyance. "You know what I'm talking about. You admitted that you can't get me out of your system."

"Are you saying I am out of yours?"

"Tell me what you've done to mitigate the damage to the other companies and people Skylar spied on through me," Jenna said rather than answer that loaded question.

"You are so sure I have done something?" he asked.

She hadn't been, but her brother's call had made Jenna take a step back from her roiling emotions and consider. "Not sure, but hopeful."

Something flicked in his gaze. Disappointment, maybe. "First, I have set our best fixers on the task of making sure that Skylar's actions follow her in her reputation, without bringing your magazine, my family or Mirrus Global into it."

Unsure how successful that endeavor could be with those caveats, Jenna nodded without enthusiasm.

This time it was easy to read the disappointment. "That does not please?"

"Let's just say I doubt how well it can work without revealing what she did to me." Jenna sighed, wondering if she was just expecting too much.

"You're assuming you are the first person she targeted this way."

Jenna had, but it was clear Dima hadn't. "You don't think I was."

"The magazine was not her first job out of university, so no."

"You think she's always done this?" Jenna's mind boggled at the idea.

Dima met her gaze, his gray eyes serious. "She was too proficient at it for you to have been the first employer she exploited."

"So you're willing to reveal another company's embarrassment?" Jenna asked, not really thrilled by that idea either.

"Rather than see you or my family hurt? Yes."

There was that streak of ruthlessness. And he showed no remorse about it either. Dima would do what he thought best.

"You were perfectly content to see me hurt," she said, not willing to let him pretend otherwise.

"No. I was not."

"Don't shine me on, Dima. When it was a choice between hurting me and protecting your royal family, you didn't hesitate."

"But I was not in any way content with the outcome. Your pain and disillusionment mattered. And that really is an admission of note if you care to take it."

CHAPTER NINE

JENNA DIDN'T ACTUALLY know what to do with Dima's admission.

If he meant it, and she thought maybe he did, then as ruthless as Dima might be, he *had* regretted hurting her when he made it a point not to regret any action he considered necessary.

"And the people she's already leaked information on?" Jenna asked, rather than dwell on something so emotionally explosive. "The ones she *still* has confidential information on that is worth selling?"

"My people went through all her electronic devices and her home for printed documentation. They took anything and everything that could be compromising to someone else. They also wiped her cloud accounts."

"She let you do that?"

"Rather than face prison? Yes."

"But you wouldn't have pressed charges."

"She could not be sure of that, could she? You did a good job convincing her you were willing to do just that, come what may."

"You used *me* as a threat?" Jenna felt a certain amount of satisfaction at that.

"Yes. Skylar also signed a confession admitting to planting the listening devices and the corporate espionage which she believes will be given to the DA if she is caught doing the same thing again."

"She could move to another state, change her name."

"She could, but she's on our radar, and she knows it."

"I…" Jenna wasn't sure exactly how she felt about all of that. "That helps."

"Good."

"But it doesn't change the fact that I couldn't do what I thought was right."

"Life is filled with compromise, and sometimes you must trust others to make sure your priorities are taken care of."

"Like you ever do that," she scoffed.

"You would be surprised at how often I've been forced to do that very thing." The look he gave her was all sober sincerity.

Jenna sighed. "I forget that you have to compromise too. Nataliya has had to often enough."

"Yes. You do not think she wanted to share the tragedy of her miscarriage with the world, do you?"

"No, I know she didn't."

And yet, even if the news hadn't been leaked early, it would have been shared. Because Nataliya's life could never be entirely private. No matter how much more comfortable that might be for the Queen of Mirrus.

He leaned back in his chair, his attention fully on Jenna, as it had been since his arrival. "So, Abu Dhabi."

She pushed her plate away and returned that attention. "You really want to go with me to the UAE?" Had he ever taken a vacation that she knew of?

Jenna couldn't remember one if he had.

"I prefer you go with me." He gave her a charming smile. "On my plane, and stay at our property there."

"You have a house in the UAE?"

"It is a condominium in an exclusive community, but yes, we have properties in most major markets."

"And it's empty right now?"

"Unless one of us is using it, the place is always empty. Allowing others to use it would be a security issue."

"That seems like a waste, doesn't it?" Even as she asked, she realized how little she cared.

She was just making conversation to give her brain a chance to process everything. The fact he'd neutralized Skylar, maybe not with the transparency Jenna would have preferred, but he'd done it all the same.

The fact he wanted sex again with her enough to go on a last-minute trip *with* her to make that happen.

Overkill?

Maybe. But better than the overkill of multiple listening devices hidden in her accessories.

"It cannot be helped," he said, a shrug in his tone.

It took her a second to remember what he was talking about. Oh, yes, responding to her question.

"Why are you doing this?" she asked, needing him to tell her again.

Maybe it would make more sense the second time around.

"I told you."

"We aren't done yet." He meant sex. "You are going on vacation, at the last minute, *you*, just so you can get more sex?"

"Not vacation exactly."

"What then?"

"I will have to work part of each day, and since I am there, I will move forward meetings that were to be scheduled with other companies for next month."

"Can they be moved?" Just because he wanted to change his travel schedule?

"It would be the best interest of the companies to do so."

"Mirrus isn't a major world power."

"No, it is a small island country with some very important natural resources. Mirrus Global, however, is a multibillion-dollar corporation with powerful connections worldwide."

"The company protects the country," she said, making sense of something she'd wondered about for a while.

How Mirrus had maintained its independence.

"Yes. We have powerful business partners with deeply felt political influence in most major markets."

"Don't you mean countries?"

"It is my brother's job to think in terms of country. I make money."

"And use it to exert influence."

"Yes, but also to build infrastructure and improve education and employment for my people."

"It doesn't bother you to use your control over money to wield power in other countries?"

"No."

"You are so sure of yourself and your path."

"Are you trying to imply you are not? Because we both know that is not true."

His words shocked her. She wasn't like that. "I'm not sure what you mean."

"You have pushed your sustainable fashion agenda to the point you are now influencing not only your magazine, but designers and even clothing manufacturers."

"I am trying to take care of our planet." And her influence at her magazine wasn't nearly as far-reaching as she would like.

Their focus was still almost entirely on traditional fast fashion.

"That is a laudable goal," he said, approval warm in his voice. "I am taking care of my country."

"You said that was your brother's job."

"No, I said it was his job to pay attention to country distinctions. It is mine to know markets."

"You're splitting hairs."

"I do not see it that way."

"Stubborn."

He gave her a devastating smile. "Like is drawn to like."

"I'm not stubborn," she lied.

"I can imagine those who know you well laughing at the hilarity of that statement."

"Maybe." She shook her head and pulled her plate back toward her, resuming eating her dinner, her appetite stronger than it had been in days.

She *was* stubborn. And liked herself that way, so she didn't see it changing.

Jenna thought too many people lived without the things that gave them joy because they were not stubborn enough. If that was a self-justification for a personality trait that could be both weakness and strength, so be it.

"We will need to have a layover in New York so I can take an in-person meeting that could not be moved."

"You're assuming I'm going to Abu Dhabi with you."

"Yes, I am."

"Arrogant."

"Undoubtedly."

"At least you didn't try to say I am too."

"You have your own arrogance, but it is tempered by your compassion."

"And yours?"

"No doubt could use some tempering."

"You're very honest with yourself and about yourself." It was one of the things that drew her to Dima.

More than his brothers, he could admit to what others might consider flaws, but maybe that was because he didn't see them as flaws?

Of course, he probably couldn't imagine anything worse than lacking confidence like any other mere mortal.

"What is that look?" he asked her.

"What look?"

"If I knew, I would not have asked."

"I was just thinking that you don't suffer from the crises of confidence that plague most of us."

They finished dinner without much more discussion, like Dima was giving her some time to think. Which surprised her, but she liked it too.

When they were done eating, Dima helped her clear the table.

"You're awfully well domesticated for a prince."

"I had no domestic help in university, graduate school or my two years of active duty in the military."

"None?" she asked doubtfully.

"None. I could have had a cleaning service, at least at university and grad school, but I wanted to experience life as most of my country's citizens do while I still had the chance of doing so."

"You went without security too?" This time she was more horrified than questioning.

"As much as possible, yes. You don't imagine I had security in my military unit. We *were* the security."

"I didn't realize. Did your brothers do the same thing?"

"Not as such."

Which means what? she wondered.

"You really want to go to Abu Dhabi together, just so we can have some more uncomplicated sex?"

"The sex so far has not been without its complications."

She could not disagree. "But the understanding still stands? We are having sex, not starting a relationship."

"We already have a relationship. We are friends, and you are part of my family."

She couldn't help the grimace that twisted her mouth.

"Don't," he ordered.

"Don't what?"

"Think your life would be better without Nataliya and the rest of us Merikovs in it."

"You don't know that's what I was thinking."

"Don't I?"

"No, Mr. Smarty-pants. I could never think my life would be *better* without my BFF." Just easier. More straightforward.

"And yet you are considering breaking off your friendship."

"Not because I think my life would be better."

"If not better, then what?"

"More honest."

"In what way is your life dishonest?"

"Not telling the people that Skylar hurt by selling information about them, that it had happened."

"You would be fired if you did so."

"You sound very sure of that." She wasn't denying it, but Jenna wasn't positive that would be the outcome either.

She hadn't been allowed to put it to the test. In the end, it hadn't been the magazine that put a gag on her.

"That kind of admission would make the magazine vulnerable to expensive liability," Dima pointed out, clearly in a different headspace about it. "Not to mention seriously undermining its reputation in the fashion industry."

"Even so, it's my relationship with you all that has taken my choices away."

"Some of them. Being born into my family took away

many of mine." He didn't sound particularly bothered by that truth.

But then he'd had an entire lifetime to come to terms with it.

"You can't change the role you were born into, but I can determine who I am friends with."

"Can you?"

"What do you mean?"

"Could you really walk away from Nataliya, who is like a sister to you, simply because the friendship isn't always convenient?" The look he gave her said he doubted it.

"I don't know." She had no trouble admitting that. "It's one of the things I planned to think about while I'm on vacation."

"One of them?"

She shrugged. "I'm in a life-assessing frame of mind right now, I guess."

"And what else do you want to assess in your life, besides your role in my family?"

"I'm not sure I want to stay at the magazine." Like usual, Jenna found it way too easy to talk to Dima.

Like her brother Luke. Only her other feelings toward Dima were anything but familial.

Shock flashed in Dima's gray gaze. "Why?"

"The industry has changed a lot in the last decade, but especially for print media." Which was an answer, but not the whole answer.

"Are you saying you've been considering this move for a while?"

"Not consciously." But what had happened with Skylar, and the magazine's reaction to it, had brought what had been nebulous feelings of discontent into stark relief.

"And subconsciously?" he asked leadingly.

"The magazine is never going to give as much attention to sustainable fashion and all size models as I want it to."

"Your activism is as important to you as your job?"

"It is," Jenna admitted, maybe even finally to herself. "I just don't know if I can make a living doing what I want to do."

She wasn't interested in being rich, but Jenna did need to provide for her own basic needs, like food and shelter.

"You were the contributing editor of a very successful adjunct blog before being promoted into your current position."

"You know a lot about me. Should I be flattered?"

"Do you know any less about me?"

"Maybe not." Jenna may have asked Nataliya more than her fair share of questions about Dima over the years.

She'd kept track of where he was and how he was doing when he was deployed. She had alerts set up for him too, and they were friends on social media.

"I'm not stalking you."

"No, you are not. We live in an information age, and keeping up with those nearest to us includes things like search engine alerts."

"Are you reading my mind?"

"I simply know what I do to keep up with my family, to keep up with you."

"You have an alert set for me?"

"And I subscribe to your magazine."

He was suspiciously as enthralled by her as she was by him. That was a dangerous situation. "We can't ever be more than friends with benefits, Dima. You know that, right?"

"We are friends. The benefits are what concern me right now. Jenna, I want you. Too damn much. If two weeks in

Abu Dhabi will get this craving out of my system, I am willing to make them happen."

Another admission she wasn't sure she would have had the courage to voice. But then, Jenna was not even going to try to convince herself that two weeks together would be enough to get Dima out of her system.

The fact that he thought it would work with him for her was both a relief and a little bit of a letdown.

"All right. I'll go."

His smile was a little predatory, and too darn sexy. "I am very pleased to hear that." He moved toward her, making the kitchen feel smaller than it was. "Perhaps we should celebrate."

"I need to pack."

"I will help you."

"You'll help me?" she asked, unable to stifle the laugh that burbled up. "This I have got to see."

"If it gets us to the celebrating more quickly, I can fold clothes with crease-free precision."

He didn't just fold clothes, but offered advice on what she should bring, and it wasn't all lingerie. Not that the man didn't have a heyday with her nightie drawer, asking oh, so casually if she wouldn't bring the blue silk chemise that barely covered her butt cheeks.

Jenna made room for the lingerie and found that packing actually went really quickly with two people putting her clothes and things together. She kept a permanently packed roll-up with all her skin products, face mask for sleeping and the like, which she tossed in her case first thing.

"I have to say, I'm impressed." Jenna surveyed her neatly packed suitcase and matching garment bag with satisfaction. "That went much faster than usual."

"Two sets of hands make light the work."

"I think that adage is *many hands*, but you are right." It was also easier because she hadn't needed to style several outfits for particular fashion events she would be attending.

Jenna had brought mostly clothes for relaxing and sightseeing, but her garment bag held three gorgeous outfits in case she and Dima decided to sample the nightlife or go out to an elite restaurant.

He'd suggested she bring at least two swimsuits since the Merikov-owned property had a private pool.

Sexually stimulating memories of her last time in a pool with him made her all too eager to comply with that request. Though honestly, Jenna questioned just how much time she would end up wearing either swimsuit.

"Now, we celebrate."

"What about your packing?" she asked even as her body moved toward him of its own volition.

He reached out and cupped her nape, his gray gaze burning her with intensity. "I have people who will do that for me."

She would have said something about it being nice to be him, but his lips were covering hers, and she was enjoying the kiss too much.

This time should have been less frantic then that first night. They'd done this before, but Jenna was starving for the feel of his skin against hers, as if it had been months, not days since they'd shared passion in his hotel room.

With the way Dima shed his clothes so quickly, he felt the same.

They fell onto the bed, not even bothering to pull the comforter back and continued their passionate kiss, their hands everywhere.

He'd learned her erogenous zones the other night and again paid them special attention while seemingly intent on showing her that she had more spots on her body that sent sensual pleasure zinging through her than she'd ever known.

She returned touch for touch, undulating against him, aching for the intimacy of joining while relearning the feel of his muscular body under her hands.

They rolled across the bed, laughing when they nearly fell off together. The laughter didn't last long in the face of their mutual sexual need, and he shifted so he was between her legs, his erection pressing against her entrance.

"Okay?" he asked.

She nodded frantically.

He didn't immediately enter her, though. "No condom?"

"We don't need one." They'd talked about it before. "Right?"

"Right."

But there was something going on here. "Why?" she asked.

"Trust."

"I trust you." In this, at least. Maybe even in a heck of a lot more.

He hadn't made her priorities to be honest to those who had been affected and to make sure Skylar couldn't just go on her way, spying on her next employer, his top consideration, but he hadn't ignored them either. Jenna could fall in love with this man if she let herself.

All thoughts of taboo emotions splintered as he pressed inside her. They moved together as if they had known this intimacy a lifetime, not a single night. She climaxed first, but only by a few seconds, and then they were heaving with spent passion together.

Jenna's eyelids were growing ridiculously heavy, but she hadn't been sleeping much lately, and right this moment, she felt safe.

She fell asleep before he pulled out of her.

* * *

Dimitri would have been insulted if any other woman had fallen asleep that fast after making love, but he'd seen the tiredness in Jenna's eyes when he arrived. He doubted she'd been sleeping these past two weeks.

Not if she was *still* considering breaking ties with his family, not to mention the career she'd spent her adult life building.

He leaned down and kissed her forehead, and then, because he simply could not help himself, her temples. Finally gave a soft buss to her passion-swollen lips.

Something in the region of his heart squeezed as he carefully disengaged from her body, and she did nothing more than give a soft sigh.

She trusted him. Probably more than she realized.

That trust was humbling.

He knew she'd felt let down when he'd reminded her of the NDA and effectively tied her hands in the matter of her assistant's spying.

Jenna had to have been devastated to find out someone she'd trusted had betrayed her so badly. Dimitri hadn't taken that into consideration at first, but after talking to Kon, he'd realized what a mistake he'd made.

Jenna's refusal to answer his calls and most of his texts had been a pretty good indicator as well. Dimitri had spent his entire life being told there were few he could trust and even fewer who would never betray him.

He hadn't accounted for the fact that Jenna had not been raised as he had been. She was not part of the royal family; she wasn't even nobility.

Her parents were not wealthy, but middle class Americans who had never even made it into the papers before their three surviving children succeeded in careers that put them at different epicenters of the public eye.

As much as he might despise it, Dimitri's own father was used to being featured in both tabloids and the legitimate press. The Merikovs were accustomed to being spied on, but that didn't mean they didn't do what they needed to in order to protect the most sensitive information in their lives and business.

Jenna had to be hurting at Skylar's betrayal. She was hurting enough at not being able to press charges and *make it right* that she was considering ending a friendship that was as close as family.

Dimitri should have considered all of that before his heavy-handed insistence she keep her own counsel about the spying.

He'd hoped his actions with her brother would show Jenna that her needs were important to him, that Dimitri cared about her emotional well-being.

Not that he made it a habit of considering that aspect of most of his friendships.

Jenna was different, though.

She was special.

And Dimitri wanted her in his bed. Permanently.

He could acknowledge that to himself, if not to the skittish fashion editor.

He'd barely kept a straight face telling her he planned to get her out of his system.

But if he'd told her the truth, that Abu Dhabi was the first volley in a princely courtship, she would have run fast and far.

Jenna didn't want to be a princess. She didn't want to get more embroiled in the lives of the Merikov family than she already was.

It was Dimitri's job to convince her differently.

Kon had done it with Emma, and frankly, Dimitri thought his brother had a lot more to overcome than he did.

Though to hear Kon tell it, the opposite was true.

Kon and Nikolai both thought that how Dimitri had handled things so far had been disastrous. Unused to being censured by his brothers, Dimitri had withdrawn from any further personal discussions while he was in Mirrus.

Until his father had cornered him and reminded him that he'd promised to attend an event where potential partners for him had been invited. Unwilling to get into who he was hoping to align his life with, Dimitri had gone.

If he was lucky, the pictures of him talking and dancing with a princess would hit the news cycle while they were in Abu Dhabi, and Jenna would never even see them.

Jenna would deny that she cared, but Dimitri did not need to remind her that his father thought other women were potential wives for him. She was skittish enough as it was, but they connected in a way he'd never thought to with a woman.

Dimitri had no desire to fall in love like his brothers.

What both Kon and Nikolai had gone through because they loved the women they'd married wasn't something Dimitri ever wanted to experience himself. He and Jenna got along well, and their sexual chemistry was off the charts. She fit in with the rest of his family and had been doing so for several years.

She was perfect for him.

Now, he just had to show her how perfect he could be for her as well.

It started with a last-minute trip to Abu Dhabi.

CHAPTER TEN

JENNA WOKE SURROUNDED by warmth and feeling more rested than she had since discovering Skylar's penchant for spying.

A heavy masculine arm rested over her body at her waist, heated strength all along her back.

She turned to face him, inhaling his scent. "Mmm..." she practically purred. "You smell good."

"I had a video meeting, so I showered."

And yet, he'd undressed again and returned to her bed. Pleasure at that knowledge coursed through her.

"When is our takeoff?"

"We have two hours. Just enough time."

"For?" As if she didn't know.

"This." He nuzzled in, kissing her neck and sending shivers of delight cascading along her nerve endings.

They barely made their takeoff time.

Jenna settled comfortably in her seat beside Dima, accepting the flight attendant's offer of her favorite bubbly water infused with citrus.

"You're used to flying by private jet," he observed.

"Only to Mirrus."

"That's a short flight."

"It is." She'd taken both jets and helicopters to the island country to visit Nataliya. "Abu Dhabi will take much longer to reach."

"With a layover in New York."

"How long will we be there?"

"We arrive this evening and fly out again tomorrow evening."

"The red-eye?"

"Better to sleep on such a long flight."

"I've never found that particularly helpful with jet lag, though I know some people do."

"Then I won't feel guilty if I keep you awake."

There could be no question what he meant by that, and Jenna wasn't complaining. Not even a little.

"I think I'll take in some sights when we're in New York."

"But you have been to the city many times."

"For Fashion Weeks, and other work-related stuff. There's never time to go to the Met, or visit the Empire State Building, or just take a harbor cruise."

"I will be finished with business by two. Save the harbor cruise for me. I will arrange everything."

"*You* will?"

"I'll have it arranged. How is that?"

"More truthful and honestly? Wonderful! I'm really looking forward to it."

His smile said he was looking forward to something too, but it had nothing to do with taking a boat ride to see the sights.

Whatever he might have rather been doing, and Jenna had little doubt what that was—her body was pleasantly sore from sensual use—Dima had to work on most of the flight. However, he'd arranged for her to view a first-run movie Jenna had mentioned she wanted to see.

The noise-canceling headphones and large screen that

dropped down from the ceiling made it a totally immersive experience.

When it was over, he asked, "Did you enjoy it?"

"Yes, very much. Only…"

"What?"

"I cannot see either you or your brothers watching movies on a long flight."

"What can you see us doing?"

"Working, just like you are right now."

"Good call. I do not believe I have ever watched a movie on a long flight. I am either sleeping or working."

"I can think of something else you could do to pass the time." She'd noticed this jet had a bedroom in the back when she'd used the restroom earlier.

"Can you?" Dima moved into her personal space, his mouth hovering over hers. "What might that be?"

"Come with me and find out," she taunted, before sliding out of her seat and away from him.

She didn't have to turn around to know he followed her. She could feel him right behind her.

The bed took up most of the small room, but it was made up with luxurious silk coverlet and sheets and piled high with pillows all the colors of the royal house. The silk duvet cover had the royal house coat of arms embroidered in the center.

An impressionist painting of the palace in Mirrus hung on the wall opposite the bed. Soft cove lighting loaned the room a romantic air, though she was sure it had been designed the way it had to encourage peaceful slumber.

The room was so clearly meant to impress and remind the occupant of the connection to the royal house.

But Jenna loved the colors and the lighting, and it just added to her sense of anticipation for what was to come.

She turned to face Dimitri. "It's so regal in here, but I don't feel like I don't belong."

"I am very glad to hear that." He shrugged out of his suit jacket and hung it up.

"Oh, very fastidious of you, Your Highness."

"Now, if you always used that tone when you call me that, it would never bother me." He tugged his tie loose. "I'm not sloppy by nature, you may have noticed, and in a room this small, there simply is no place for haphazardly discarded clothing."

"Why do I find it charming you think about stuff like that? I should be offended you're more worried about the aesthetics of the room than you are about getting naked with me."

"Perhaps because you know with certainty that there is *nothing* short of family or country emergency that takes precedence over that with me."

"You know? I believe you."

He continued undressing but gave her a heated look.

Jenna took that as her cue to get rid of her own clothes. Following his example, she hung them up in the closet. She was reaching around her back to unhook her bra when she felt hands there, helping her.

"Your skin is so soft, silky and warm." His hands brushed over her back.

Shivers cascaded down her spine, her body shaking with desire so strong, her knees wanted to give way.

He reached around and cupped both her breasts as she pulled her bra away and let it drop. Uncluttered floors not making it on her list of priorities in the moment.

He brushed over her nipples, awakening pleasure with the first touch. After their lovemaking the night before and that morning, Jenna's skin was super sensitized. Her nipples beaded with pleasure that bordered on pain. Atavistic anticipation sent throbbing warmth between her legs.

Dimitri pressed her nipples between his thumbs and forefingers, gently squeezing and releasing before rolling them.

Every tiny touch sent ecstasy shooting to her very core, and Jenna was ready for him before they even lay down on the bed. He hadn't even touched her clitoris, but Jenna knew climax was imminent.

He seemed to know too, because Dimitri pulled her to the bed, laying her down before disappearing between her legs, his mouth working sensual magic that had her crying out in seconds.

She'd had three orgasms by the time he came inside her, his shout triumphant.

She couldn't even begrudge him that victorious sound. He'd conquered her body like an invading army intent on building up rather than destroying.

Wrecked, Jenna snuggled into Dima like she never did with men in her bed and slipped once again into slumber without a second thought.

Dima's penthouse apartment was all modern and sleek. That did not surprise Jenna.

How at home she felt in it did.

"Your artwork is amazing." The paintings on the wall were not anonymous prints, but carefully chosen pieces that reflected both his taste and the aesthetic of the apartment.

One was by an artist Jenna knew only put out two to three pieces a year, all of which sold for at least a high six figures. She knew that because the artist was one of her favorites and entirely out of her price range.

"I didn't realize you were an art collector," Jenna said,

doing nothing to hide her admiration for the beautiful pieces that graced his walls.

Dima was sifting through a stack of papers his admin had greeted him with at the airport. He dictated instructions into his phone for some and signed others.

He placed one in the flat document box he was using for them all as he finished with them. "I know what I like."

"What you like is high-end and high-quality."

"I am glad you approve." He dropped the last sheaf into the box and flipped the lid shut, then turned to face her. "I believe art is an extension of not only the creator, but the person who seeks to possess it."

"I agree. You have excellent taste."

He gave her one of those heated looks that sent her nerve endings zinging. "I would say your presence here is a testament to that."

"You're very complimentary."

"Honest. Jenna, I am honest. You are a unique and intriguing woman."

"I'm just me."

"I like you."

"I've noticed." She smiled. "I like you too."

"Not when I'm stopping you doing what you think is right."

That was Dima, a man confident enough in himself he would never shy away from talking about the hard stuff.

"Not so much then, no."

"Do you want to eat dinner out, or have something delivered?" he asked, clearly uninterested in belaboring the point.

Jenna kicked off her shoes, feeling a certain satisfaction in mussing up his perfect living space just that little bit, and headed into his state-of-the-art kitchen. "Do you have anything to cook?"

"I doubt it. My housekeeper keeps my favorite beverages and sandwich makings stocked."

"So much for being domesticated. You have all this—" she indicated the kitchen a chef would envy "—and you only use it for snacks and drinks."

"Yes." Dima didn't seem embarrassed by the admission either.

"Did you cook for yourself during university and graduate school?"

"I did, but I have no time to do so now and no one to cook for besides myself. Most of my meals are taken up with business meetings and are either catered or at restaurants."

"You're awfully fit for all that eating out."

"I work out every day, and I use farm-to-table caterers."

"What about lovers?"

"What about them?"

"Do you at least cook for them? Or let them cook for you?" Jenna loved cooking to relax, following along with her favorite celebrity chefs as best she could.

"I don't do lovers. Therefore I do not cook for them."

He wasn't a monk. So, what was he saying?

"Then what am I? A friend with benefits," she said, answering her own question.

But he shook his head. "We will call it by its name. This is not cute, casual sex together when no one else is available."

"You're not an afterthought," she agreed. He was the one man she wanted badly enough to ignore her own rules and even her instinct for self-preservation.

"You are my lover, Jenna. And until you tell me otherwise, you will be the only woman in my bed."

"Same." She wasn't going to belabor the point, not least

of which because the knowledge wasn't something *she* wanted to dwell on.

"Good to know."

"If we eat out, can we go someplace totally touristy, like a celebrity chef restaurant or something?" she asked as much because she hungry as she wanted to change the subject.

"You're really intent on making this a full-on vacation, aren't you?"

"Yes," she responded without apology.

The only vacation time she'd taken in ten years was for family stuff. The only travel she'd done was for work. These two weeks were going to be neither.

No family stuff. No work. Jenna was going to play tourist to the hilt.

"Freshen up, and I'll get us a table somewhere."

"You will?" she teased, not sure why she always pushed that point.

Was it because she needed the reminder that he had staff to do stuff like that for him, and she did not? That they came from completely disparate worlds?

Despite her friendship with his queenly sister-in-law, Jenna herself was not royal, or rich, or even moderately famous. Her brother was more well-known by the media.

Both Jenna and Nataliya liked it that way.

"I will call my people."

"Okay." She gave him a cheeky grin and then headed off to find the bedroom and the en suite bathroom so she could do what he suggested.

Freshen up.

She'd like to think the time away from him might give her some perspective, but she knew that was a lost cause. She had not just had sex with the prince, but even more telling, Jenna had fallen asleep on the man. Twice.

Feeling secure like she never did, and after the past weeks, that was really strange. Like really, *really* strange.

He'd hidden things from her, forced her to back off on her own sense of integrity and hurt her. Yet she still trusted him on a deep, visceral level that allowed her to rest with him when sleep had been so hard to come by otherwise.

She'd like to believe she'd just been tired enough and the sex had relaxed her sufficiently to make it happen. But that wouldn't account for the sense of well-being Jenna had both before falling asleep and upon waking.

Dimitri smiled at Jenna's delighted response as the driver pulled their car into the spot in front of the building where one of her favorite celebrity chefs had a restaurant. Getting a table was usually at least a month-long wait, but he had strings to pull and no compunction about tugging them. Hard.

"I'd say I can't believe you got us in here, but I can."

"So doing so doesn't impress you?" he asked as he helped her out of the car, subtly maneuvering his driver out of the way to do so.

"Did I say that?" Jenna gave him a wide-eyed smile. "I'm *very* impressed and really, really pleased you were thoughtful enough to pick this restaurant."

He *had* pushed for this particular eatery when his social assistant had told him it would be easier to get a table at a different one. "The chef owed my brother a favor. I cashed it in."

"Which brother?" Jenna asked suspiciously.

"Does it matter?"

"I'm still angry with Prince Konstantin."

"I told you, he never really suspected you."

"Sure."

"You two are going to have to talk."

"Not for the next two weeks, we aren't."

"But won't knowing with certainty that he didn't suspect you impact your decision about your friendship with our family?"

"Nataliya is my BFF, not the rest of you."

They'd entered the building, and his security made sure they were the only occupants of the elevator taking them to the rooftop restaurant.

"But over the years, you have forged friendships with all of us. You and Emma are almost as close as you and Nataliya."

"Well, despite her taste in men, she's a wonderful person."

Dima ran his finger down her beautiful jaw, reveling in how she shivered at that small contact. "Now, see, I can't tell if you are teasing as you usually do about Kon, or are serious."

"Oh, really? You can't tell?" Jenna asked, sounding far too pleased by that state of affairs.

"No."

"You are more likely to influence my feelings about staying in the royal orbit than your brother. You do realize that, don't you?"

Dimitri felt those words like a punch to his heart. "No, I had not realized."

"This between us might not be long-term." She leaned up and kissed the corner of his mouth. "But it isn't *nothing* either."

He turned and caught her mouth in a real kiss, deeply satisfied when she melted into him. Definitely not nothing. And he thought it was going to be long-term, but he was smart enough to use his mouth to deepen the kiss rather than say that out loud.

The sound of a throat clearing reminded Dimitri that

they were not alone. He broke the kiss and felt his lips curve into a smile at the sight of Jenna looking disoriented from the connection. She turned him on by walking into a room. It was only fair he should impact her body with equal urgency.

The restaurant's decor was exactly like Jenna had seen on television, the clientele dressed by designers she knew well.

Jenna was used to seeing celebrities and dignitaries alike in her job and her role as a queen's BFF, but seeing one of her favorite actors out with a group of friends still required concentration not to gawp.

It did not help that Dima had kissed her silly in the elevator.

A bouquet of yellow irises graced their table, a standing ice bucket with chilling champagne beside it. Jenna wanted to remain unmoved by the show of romance, but she couldn't.

After showing kind of spectacularly that he was not as aware of her feelings as she would have liked, it meant a lot that Dima had taken the time to have the flowers delivered. It indicated that he *did* think of her when he wasn't with her.

How far that would take them, she did not know.

They had no future, but neither did she want their time together marred by incidents like the ones that had hurt her so badly already.

Dima pulled her chair out for her before taking his own.

It was all over-the-top, and in her secret heart, Jenna loved the sense of wooing and romance.

She reached out to touch an iris petal. "These are my favorite spring flowers."

"I know."

"How?"

"You are not the only one who notices things."

"You think I'm observant?" she asked him, feeling pleased and not really sure why.

"I do. If you wanted to sell secrets, you would have so many more at your disposal tucked away in your agile brain."

"That's a compliment, I think." Not that he was gaining points in the boyfriend column with bringing up that particular issue.

"It is."

"Thank you." She sighed, realizing she wasn't going to stay silent about his lack of tact, though. "Bringing up the situation that made me wonder if I wanted to ever see you again isn't your best move right now."

"I cannot pretend to be other than I am."

"What does that mean?"

"You cannot be with me only because you've chosen to ignore the harder side of spending time with a prince. This thing between us has no chance in those circumstances."

"This thing between us?" she asked carefully, suddenly feeling that an emotional minefield surrounded her.

"Whatever you want to call it, we are friends. We are having sex. I don't want to lose either of those things because another situation arises that shows the limits being connected to a family like mine brings."

"You are so unapologetic about those limits."

"On the contrary. I feel regret just like the next man."

"But you still do what you need to."

"Some consider me ruthless."

"I am sure they do."

"And you? Do you think I am ruthless?"

"I think you can be." She just had to decide if she could

live with the knowledge that ruthlessness could be turned on her, just like anyone else.

"Does it help to know that whenever possible, I will give you what *you* need?"

"This is getting really heavy for a relationship based on sex." She said it quietly, not wanting to be overheard.

"And friendship."

"But *not* friends with benefits." He'd been adamant that did not describe them adequately.

"No. We have a commitment to exclusivity until we agree that we don't." His words were no different than they had been at his penthouse.

But suddenly they felt weightier, like that *until they both agreed they didn't* clause was some kind of long-term commitment. Was that because of his attitude, or hers?

Jenna was very much afraid that the feeling of emotional weight came from inside her.

Needing a moment, Jenna picked up her menu and began perusing the offerings. Dishes she'd seen prepared, some she'd never heard of, all sounding beyond delicious.

Dima pressed down on the menu with his hand, his expression telling her he knew exactly what she was doing. And typically, in Dima fashion, he was pushing past the barrier. "We can order off the menu, or we can allow the chef to decide."

Shock coursed through her. "He's here?" Jenna looked around furtively, sure she hadn't seen the celebrated chef when they arrived.

"He is. We are sitting at a table he reserved for us, in fact."

It had been a long time since Jenna had fangirled out, but she was on the verge. She was sitting at her favorite chef's table. "That is so cool."

"I am glad that you think so." Humor laced his tone.

She made a face at him. "You're too sophisticated to get excited about stuff like this?"

"Not at all. My celebrity crushes aren't chefs, though."

"You have celebrity crushes? You?" Who would an Adonis crush on?

"Sure. Doesn't everybody?"

Right until this very minute, she would have said *no*. "So, spill."

"You are acknowledging, then, that the owner of this establishment is yours?" he asked.

Heat climbed the back of her neck, but she nodded. "I do so acknowledge."

His sexy smile reminded her that crushes were all well and good, but real-life passion was something else entirely. Something she never wanted to give up.

Which did not change the unalterable fact that at some point she would have to.

"Queen Bey."

Jenna stared in amazement for several seconds. "Beyoncé? She's your celebrity crush?" To be fair, the pop star was a lot of people's crush, but he was a prince. "I didn't know you even knew who she was."

"Everyone knows Queen Bey. Even a prince. I've seen her in concert."

"You have not."

"I did."

Jenna guessed she didn't need to worry about him getting serious over *them*. Not when his feminine ideal was that beautiful and talented.

Mere mortal women could not measure up.

"You've got a *look* again."

"I was just thinking that would be a lot to live up to for a woman who wanted a relationship with you."

"Worried, *milaya moy*? Don't be. No fantasy could live up to the very real pleasure between us."

Jenna opened her mouth to assure him she was *not* worried, but a British voice asking how they were doing froze her vocal cords.

She knew that voice.

She turned her head in what felt like slow motion to see the man in the flesh.

He was wearing his chef's whites, his face creased in a smile.

Jenna nearly swallowed her tongue.

"I was just asking Jenna if she wanted to order off the menu, or let you choose our food."

"Is there really a question?" the chef asked, raising a single brow like she'd never been able to do.

"No. I...you *want* to?"

"Of course. It is my pleasure to feed my friends, and I count the Merikov princes among them."

"He said he had to call in a favor to get the table." Jenna slapped her hand over her mouth.

But both men were laughing.

"The favor was me staying long enough to make your food personally. My table is always at his and his brothers' disposal."

"Oh," Jenna breathed. Dima had arranged for the chef to be there, to cook for her.

"I think you made major brownie points with that move, son."

"Well, then I guess it was a good thing you could stay up long enough to cook our dinner, old man."

Listening to the two tease back and forth was surreal, and really, really cool. Jenna couldn't believe she was getting the chance to do just that, much less that her favorite chef ever was going to make her dinner.

The food was amazing, but Dima's company was the best part of the night. Not that she was going to tell him that.

The man had enough personal confidence.

"I am not sure if it will be me in your bed tonight, or dreams of your crush," he teased her as she swooned over dessert.

She shook her head, too serious about this to tease. "It can only ever be you if you are the one that is there, Dima."

She'd wanted him so long. How many sexy times dreams had she had about this man? Even more disturbing, how many regular life dreams had she had about him?

Despite the sure and certain knowledge she would never have a child, she had dreamed about having a baby with him every few months for the past few years. She'd never told a soul. Not Nataliya. Not Luke or Lisa.

It was no use sharing dreams that could never come true.

And Jenna had no desire to be pitied.

CHAPTER ELEVEN

THAT NIGHT THEY made love in the shower, but Jenna went to bed alone because Dima had work he had to do.

She woke in the middle of the night to his naked body wrapped around hers, and it felt so right. She could have pulled away on principle.

It wasn't supposed to feel this good to sleep with another person. In fact, Jenna had never liked having someone else in her bed. Not a lover, not a friend, not her sister.

She liked her space, but with Dima, she gravitated to him in her sleep.

Deciding it wasn't worth worrying about when they only had two weeks together, she snuggled in and let herself go back to sleep.

Jenna next woke to an empty bed beside her, but the sound of the shower running indicated Dima hadn't been gone long. She threw back the covers and padded naked into the bathroom.

He stood under the shower, hot water cascading down over his golden body.

Jenna throbbed between her legs, her nipples beading with need.

He turned, like he knew she was there, and his welcoming smile drew her like a magnet.

Jenna stepped into the shower and right into a good-morning kiss that curled her toes.

They didn't have penetrative sex but used their hands to give one another pleasure before he jumped out, reminding her to save the harbor cruise for him.

Jenna stood under the hot water way too long for conscience's sake. She wasn't saving any dolphins with this long shower.

Grimacing at the thought, she finally turned off the water and got out to dry off. She had the whole morning to sightsee, and she planned to make the most of it.

She discovered that Dima had left a car and driver at her disposal. Jenna took advantage, loving that this driver was both friendly and clearly enamored of his adopted city. He told her stories about many of the buildings they passed as well as his own life in New York.

He insisted she have a hot dog from a vendor for lunch. Jenna was so glad she did. She'd never had one with that much flavor and dressed so perfectly.

At two o'clock, he took her to the harbor, but not the docks where the boats that hosted the harbor cruises were moored.

This dock had row after row of yachts.

A man dressed in crisp sailor blues stepped forward to open her door when the driver pulled the luxurious sedan to a stop beside the curb.

He offered her a hand out of the car. "Miss Beals, His Highness is waiting for you on the yacht."

She accepted the man's help but turned to lean back into the car. "Thank you so much, Jackie. You gave me a wonderful tour of the city today. I've never seen it in the same way all the times I've been here for Fashion Week."

"It was my pleasure, Jenna." He winked. "My sister is

going to think I'm a hero when I give her those tickets to Fashion Week you arranged for me."

"I'm glad. Tell her to shoot me an email and let me know what she thought." Jenna knew a budding fashion designer would leap at the chance to talk to someone with her contacts.

And she was happy to help when she could.

Jackie was fantastic as a driver for Mirrus Global but was only doing it while he finished up his engineering degree.

His younger sister had different aspirations. She'd already gotten into a top fashion design school, and that showed Jenna the young woman was serious about pursuing a career as a designer.

Jenna remembered that time in her life when she'd been going to university for her degree in journalism. She'd had so many plans for what she wanted to do with it, and honestly? Jenna had achieved her goals.

Now she was thirty-five and wondering if she needed new dreams to pursue.

She followed the sailor to a large gleaming yacht. Stepping aboard, she looked around for Dima, but was unsurprised not to find him on the deck.

Most likely he was getting some work in while waiting.

The sailor led her to a large living room where she did indeed find Dima working away on his laptop.

However, he looked up immediately upon her entrance, and his expression said he was glad to see her. "Hello, *milaya moy*. Did you have a good day?"

"It was fantastic. Jackie is an amazing guide to the city, and that young man is wicked smart."

"He'll make a good engineer."

"You know who he is?" she asked, surprised.

Dima's dark brows drew together. "You think I would

send you out in the city for the day with someone I did not?"

"If I say yes, will that get me in trouble?"

"No trouble, but let me assure you that it is true." His tone said maybe a *little* trouble.

"I believe you now. I just would not have thought that before," she said in all honesty.

He stood up and moved toward her. "You do not think enough of your own importance."

"It's not that I don't think I'm important. It's that I can't be that important to *you*." Still, she didn't move away from him, did she?

He stopped so his big body was only a breath away from hers. "There you are wrong, Jenna. You are very important to me."

"Watch it," she said, fear making her voice harsh. "We aren't in that kind of relationship, Dima."

"Jenna, the number of people allowed to call me that name is a very short list and includes only family." He cupped her nape, his expression showing no hint of humor. "Yet you are on it. What kind of relationship do you think we need for you to be important to me?"

"I just…this can't be more than what it is."

"Why is that?" He brushed his lips over hers.

"I…" Telling him would build the intimacy between them. Not telling him could leave him believing there was a chance.

Only, they'd agreed they weren't doing anything more than sex.

She stepped back from him, forcing his hands to drop from her neck. "Why are we having this discussion? We agreed this was just sex."

Why did it feel like she was running?

"But we are also friends. Whatever makes you think

you cannot have a life with me, or amongst my family, is naturally of concern to me."

"You speak so formally sometimes."

"I admit it. That is in fact a prince thing, as you like to call it." His eyes teased her.

"I figured." She bit her lip, thinking.

Talk, or don't talk?

"Tell me."

"What?" She gave him her best guileless look.

The look was wasted on him. He just stared at her, clearly unwilling to allow prevarication about this.

She sighed, part of her wanting to share her past and part of her knowing that no matter how many years had passed, it never stopped hurting to do so.

"I'm not the oldest child in my family." That's where it started. With her brother, Matt.

He took her hand and led her to the large horseshoe-shaped sofa. "I thought you were." Dima sat down and despite all that room, pulled her into his lap.

"No. Matt was two years older than me." She let her head rest against his chest. This was easier to talk about without making eye contact. "He was the best big brother. He never made me feel like I was in the way."

Dima's arms tightened around her. "What happened to him?"

"He got sick when I was ten. At first, we didn't know what it was, you know?" Pain welled, like it always did. "But it turns out that my mom carried a gene for a degenerative disease."

Dima went very still. "Your mother is not sick."

"Neither am I."

He let out a breath she hadn't realized he was holding. "However, you *do* have this gene?"

"Yes." Inactive, but there in her genetic makeup, just

waiting to be passed on to the next generation, which she would never allow. "Matt died when I was sixteen after years of pain and slowly, inexorably losing more and more of himself to the disease."

"I am very sorry."

Jenna nodded, acknowledging the sincerity of his sentiment. "We were all tested for it." She lifted her head so their gazes met. "I was the only other child carrying the gene."

"Could you still get sick?"

"No. It would have come on during adolescence. It didn't, but my parents were watching for it. We were all scared, though, until I aged past the window when it would have manifested." Looking back, she realized how that had shaped her and her siblings.

Her parents too. Though she honestly didn't remember what they'd been like before Matt had gotten sick. Her memory had melded it all together.

But her brother Luke had gone from being a determined boy to a driven man who'd built nothing short of an empire by the time he was thirty. Lisa, their baby sister, had rejected college and gotten married young, having four children in six years. She and her husband were happy living their organic, off-the-grid lifestyle.

"Explain why this terrible tragedy means you and I cannot have a future."

"I had a tubal ligation the day after my twenty-first birthday."

"So that you could not pass on this gene that had wreaked such terrible pain on your family," he guessed.

Though he sure sounded like he had no doubt about being right.

"It took my brother from me. I could never risk it taking a child. Also, it stops with me. This disease will not make it to the next generation of my family."

"No cousins who have it?"

"Only one, and he took the same permanent measures, having a vasectomy."

"You are both very courageous."

"I didn't feel courageous at twenty-one. I felt desperate." She'd still been grieving the loss of her brother.

He rubbed her back, the touch consoling and yet...enticing too.

So much about Dima and her feelings for him were like that. Complicated.

"So you cannot get pregnant by conventional means."

"I *will not* get pregnant by any means."

"That is your choice."

She relaxed against him. "Yes."

"And this is why you believe we have no future."

"The main reason, but there are others."

"I am a prince."

"That is one of them."

"What are the others?" he asked, not sounding particularly stressed by her revelations.

So he hadn't been thinking of a future with her. Not really.

But Dima, being Dima, wanted to know everything.

"You're younger than me."

"Five years at our ages hardly matters. Both my brothers have a bigger age gap with their wives."

"It's not the same."

"In what way?"

"Everyone accepts that kind of thing when the man is older."

His laughter shocked her.

She sat up in offense. "What's so funny?"

"I never thought I would live to see the day that a die-hard feminist like yourself would make a statement like that."

"I didn't say I felt that way."

"Then what does it matter what others think?"

"The tabloids are going to have a field day with us as it is. Can you imagine if we got engaged?"

"I do not live my life by what the tabloids decide to print about me."

"Really? You've worked really hard to stay out of them, especially since Galena's very public split with you."

"None of us likes to be featured in the gutter press, but I'm not going to live my life by giving up what I want to avoid it."

"Clearly, or you wouldn't be going to Abu Dhabi with me."

"Exactly."

"Still, a lover is not the same thing as a potential partner."

"Sometimes they are one and the same."

"Well, now is not one of those times."

"So you say."

"And so you should know as well, Dima. I can't give you children, and even if I could, I wouldn't want my children growing up in a palace."

"I do not live in a palace. I live in a penthouse."

She opened her mouth to argue, but he forestalled her with a kiss.

A very nice, thought-stealing move of his lips over hers with just a tiny swipe of his tongue along the seam of her lips before he pulled back. "Kon and Emma do not live in a palace either."

"They do part of the year."

"They visit Mirrus. That is not the same thing."

"If you say so."

"I do."

"Okay."

"You can be maddening, Jenna."

"You think so? I thought I was just being pragmatic."

He shook his head, but he didn't say anything. Just stood up, lifting her with him, and headed out of the room.

"Where are we going?"

"I would like it to be bed, but in fact we are headed for the observation deck. Your harbor cruise has started."

The yacht was moving, and Jenna hadn't even noticed, she was so intent on her conversation with Dima.

He let her down when they reached the deck. A voice sounded over the state-of-the-art speaker system, giving a running commentary on the landmarks that could be seen from the water as well as tidbits of New York history she had never heard.

She and Dima stood at the rail for the first hour, taking everything in, but eventually they moved to sit together on an outdoor love seat, where they sipped their bubbly water and enjoyed the views while their bodies touched from shoulder to thigh.

It was odd.

And Jenna wasn't sure how she felt about that. Nataliya was bound to learn about the shared vacation.

Jenna had a hard time believing Dima was willing to feature in gossip columns for the chance at spending this time together.

And yet, hadn't he said he would be working her out of his system?

"What other objections do you have to a relationship with me?" he asked, like their conversation had not paused for the tour.

"The last couple of weeks have been brutal. I cannot imagine a lifetime of compromising my integrity."

"That is a harsh indictment."

"You did hear me say the last two weeks have been brutal?"

He didn't reply, but then the question had been rhetorical.

Jenna got lost in the commentary of the tour once again, so another hour passed before she realized it. They were pulling into a slip near the Statue of Liberty.

"What are we doing?" she asked.

"You said you wanted to play tourist. Nothing could be more iconic than the Statue of Liberty."

A prince visiting the Statue of Liberty was a little different than the average person. They didn't shut it down or anything. She didn't imagine they had time to arrange it, but the bodyguards managed to create space around them. When they got inside, he'd arranged for access all the way up the ladder to the inside of the flame.

There was a small hatch they climbed through to the walkway used to service the spotlights that were directed at the flame at night.

Wind whipped Jenna's blond hair around her head and her clothes around her body, but the view was magnificent.

"This is incredible." She had to practically shout to be heard.

Dima wrapped an arm around her, pulling her in to his body. "It is impressive."

Jenna felt safe in his arms, regardless of the wind and the way it felt like the narrow platform swayed under her feet.

"Your Highness." That was all the security head said.

But the way Dima's body stiffened told her he knew what the prompt meant. "We have to go down again, *mi-*

laya. I did not give them enough time to arrange proper security protocols, so we have to keep the visit short."

Jenna didn't mind. She loved that he'd made this happen at all. The climb down was a heck of a lot easier than the climb up had been. When they got back out to the plaza, she stared up at the statue. "It feels heavy being here."

"I imagine it does." He took her hand, uncaring of all the people surrounding them with camera phones. "I feel a great profundity when I stand inside the original home built by my family."

"It wasn't the palace?" she asked.

"No. When my family left Russia, they did so in secret and with few of their possessions."

"So there's a log cabin out there somewhere your ancestors lived in?"

"Not a log cabin, but nothing like a palace either. It was turned into a museum after the palace was built by my great-grandfather."

"I never knew."

"I am surprised Nataliya has never spoken of it. She has taken a personal interest in preserving the history of our country."

Jenna had known that, but her BFF had never mentioned the house turned museum. "I'd like to see it."

"I will take you the next time we are in Mirrus."

She pointed out that chances were they wouldn't be there together. If she ever returned to the small island country.

Dima insisted on having their photo taken in the middle of the plaza, like all the other tourists. Of course, unlike the other tourists, their picture was taken by a bodyguard, while the other three managed a decent gap between her and Dima and the rest of the people intent on visiting the Statue of Liberty.

They made it back to the yacht, and Jenna didn't mind that Dima led her back inside. She kicked off her shoes and sat on the sofa, her legs curled under her. "I'm wiped."

Dima gave some instructions to someone just outside the door before joining her. "No club before we fly out?"

"No." The very idea of pounding bass and crushing bodies made her shiver in revulsion. "I need some downtime."

"You are not a party girl."

"Never have been. I spend Fashion Weeks *on* or holed up in my hotel room, rejuvenating."

"You're so honest. I like that about you."

"You're the same."

"And?" he prompted, sitting beside her.

"I like it too, as if you didn't know."

"Considering how much you do *not* like about me, affirmation of what you do is not a bad thing."

"What are you talking about?"

"I am a prince. I am ruthless. I am rich. I am royal."

"Prince and royal are the same thing."

"You've mentioned it in regard to both roles."

"I never said I didn't like you." Even when she'd been hurting so badly.

"Not in so many words."

"Not in any words."

"That is good to know."

She was totally lost as far as this conversation went, and just on the side of too tired and mentally exhausted to figure it out.

Dima patted his own thigh. "Here."

"Here what?" she asked.

"Your feet. You should have worn tennis shoes today."

"My sandals were perfectly comfortable." For the first hours of sightseeing anyway. Her feet ached now.

"Give them to me."

"You asked for it." She wasn't turning down a foot rub, even by a prince.

Maybe especially by a prince.

It turned out that Prince Dimitri of Mirrus gave a magnificent foot massage.

"How soon will we be back at the dock?" she asked.

"We'll have dinner on board and then dock in time to make our flight."

"I didn't repack before leaving your apartment this morning."

"My people will take care of it."

"I should insist on doing it for myself."

"Why?"

"Because I'm an independent woman."

"Allowing someone else to repack your things compromises that how?"

"It doesn't?"

"I should hope not. I am a man who makes his own decisions, but am content to allow others to do things for me if it saves me time to do what I am best at."

"Dominating the business world?"

"Only on days that end in a *y*."

The joke was old, but she laughed anyway. Because it was also true.

"You're not dominating the business world right now."

"No. I am giving you a much-needed foot rub."

"You're very good at it."

"I took a course on massage during my university days."

"Why?"

"I was dating a woman who told me that if a man was serious about giving pleasure in the bedroom, he had to learn to give pleasure out of it."

"She sounds pretty sure of herself."

"I am drawn to strong women."

"I guess so. You're going on vacation with me." Jenna had no doubts about her own inner strength.

"That I am." His massage technique changed.

Jenna started having some very different responses to Dima's moving fingers. "Please tell me this yacht has a bedroom."

"Need a shower before dinner, *milaya moy*?"

"After."

"After?" he teased as his fingers did something that went straight to her core.

Jenna gasped and jerked, but did she pull her foot away? No, she did not.

His laughter was low and oh, so very sexy.

"Dima, we need to take this someplace no one is going to walk in on us."

He nodded without any more teasing, the sexual energy coming off of him intense and powerful.

He stood up and offered his hand.

She took it without hesitation.

He led her out of the living room, down a hall and a set of stairs that ended in a set of double doors. He opened one and pulled her inside.

The cabin was as luxurious a bedroom as any she had ever seen, including the one she stayed in at the palace. Spacious and decorated with warm, rich colors and fabrics, it screamed wealth and privilege.

In another situation, Jenna would probably find it over-the-top, but in that moment, she was only thankful it had a door that could be shut and locked.

Which they did before wrecking the bed in a way she would have been certain only thirty minutes before she was too tired to do.

CHAPTER TWELVE

THEY DID TAKE a shower before dinner, and Jenna was delighted to find that he'd had her cases put on the yacht before her arrival.

She changed into a loose maxi dress that clung to her in elegant lines but would also be comfortable for travel later.

Dima's eyes warmed with approval before he crossed the room to kiss her. "Time to eat, but I would rather muss the bed again."

Staff had come in while they were in the shower, and the bed looked as pristine as when they first arrived. "That is kind of scary, you know?"

"Scary?"

"Having staff so efficient they change the bed while you are in the shower."

Dima made a noncommittal sound, but it was clear he was used to that kind of invasive pampering.

Jenna wondered if she could get used to it and shook her head.

"What are you saying no to in your mind?" he asked, showing yet again how good he was at reading her.

She was always pleased when he was stumped at what she was thinking.

"I don't think I could get used to having staff that invasively efficient."

"So give instructions for them not to enter our quarters when we are still in them." He said it like that was a no-brainer.

"I can't give instructions to your staff."

"Of course you can."

"I wouldn't feel right."

"Jenna, we are going to be spending two weeks together in Abu Dhabi. If you do not make your wishes known to the staff, it will not be the vacation either of us wants it to be."

"You said you weren't taking a vacation."

"Only working a few hours a day *is* vacation for me."

"You are a workaholic."

"Hmm…and what does that make you?"

"My family says I am a workaholic." Especially Lisa, who was content to live by the schedule of the farm but found any other pressure to conform to a calendar or time-table anathema.

"You are driven."

"I have been. Luke is worse."

"He would have had to put in hours longer than even I do to build his company as quickly as he did."

"I worry about him."

"Why exactly?"

"You think you know, but you want to hear what I say," she guessed. She loved…*liked* that about him. He might think he could read her mind, but he still asked.

"Yes."

"He's so determined to build an empire; he forgets that his life is more than his company."

"Perhaps for him, it isn't."

"He lost one marriage because of it."

"He was married?"

"Yes. He married his high school sweetheart right out

of college, but two years later, she left." Luke hadn't had a relationship since.

He didn't date. If he had lovers, he was discreet about them.

"You worry about him being alone?"

"Not really. That's Mom and Dad's job, and they harp on it enough for both of us, but I do worry he's going to have a heart attack before forty from the stress of his lifestyle."

"Have you talked to him about it?"

"No. I know he works out, has a personal chef focused on nutrition. I just..."

"Worry. You are a good sister."

"I love him." She would not lose another brother.

"Family."

Jenna smiled. "You sound like yours gives you fits."

"Can you doubt it?"

"No." She knew how pushy his father, the former king, could be.

And his brothers were every bit as arrogant as he was. Being the youngest in that crowd could not be easy, but Dima held his own.

A huge bouquet of irises, these purple, were on the sideboard by the table.

Jenna felt moisture well in her eyes, unsure why it touched her so much. "You got me flowers, again."

"You like flowers."

"I do. Especially irises this time of year, as you know."

"Yes."

"But..."

"What?"

"You keep getting me these really gorgeous bouquets."

"They are a small symbol of the value I place on your company."

"You're a romantic guy, Dima. Who knew?"

"Blame my father. He passed that trait down to all his sons."

"Even Prince Konstantin?" she asked doubtfully.

"Don't tell me that Emma has never mentioned it."

"She says your brother spoils her. I've always been skeptical."

"Jenna."

She laughed. "I'm just teasing. Mostly." She took the chair Dima pulled out for her. "He would go into shock if I stopped."

"You could be right, but know that he values your friendship, not only to his wife and sister-in-law, but to himself and the care you show his children. He speaks of you as an aunt to them."

"Putting a plug in for me staying on the periphery of the royal family?" she asked with some humor.

"Something like that."

They talked about everything from history to the latest scientific discoveries over dinner. Jenna enjoyed Dima's intelligent conversation but liked the way he respected her opinions and actively listened to her even more.

This man might be used to bossing people around, but he'd been raised to respect women, and Jenna thought maybe his father deserved recognition for doing such a good job. But the person sparking emotion in her heart she'd been so determined not to feel?

That was all Dima.

As they sat on the deck watching the city lights sparkle like manmade stars, the answer to why Jenna had agreed to travel with Dima, why she wanted this time with him regardless of what being with him had already cost her emotions, became too big to ignore.

Jenna had never been in love. She'd had relationships,

but none worth making the compromises necessary to keep them going.

Because that all-consuming feeling had not been there. Love.

Looking at Dima hurt in the best way. Touching Dima brought pleasure that had nothing to do with sex. Being touched by the prince did the same.

Sex with him was so mind-shattering, it would be easy to dismiss her feelings as sensual thrall. Only, they weren't having sex right now. They weren't even touching, and yet the connection between them was stronger than corded steel.

She didn't just want Dima. She needed him.

As terrifying as that reality was, even more so was the tiny kernel of hope that maybe, just maybe, they could make this thing between them work. Despite the fact he was a prince. Despite her age and sterility.

Her practical mind told her not to be a fool, but her heart thrummed with a love so deep she wasn't sure it had an end.

She had been slowly and surely falling in love with this man for eight years. Taking him as a lover had only cemented those feelings, making them permanent and inescapable. And no amount of telling herself it was a bad idea was going to change that.

His reaction to her list of reasons why they could not be together was ambiguous at best. If he *were* interested in a long-term relationship, shouldn't he have tried to convince her that what she saw as barriers weren't?

He hadn't seemed upset, *but* he had brought the subject up a second time to make sure he had the complete list.

Why?

Jenna had no more of an answer to that question as they boarded his private jet later than when she'd first asked it.

They'd had time to cruise the harbor and enjoy the view of the Statue of Liberty lit before docking and taking a limousine to the airport. The whole time, they'd talked about anything and everything, except the one thing Jenna could not stop thinking about.

Was Dima still set on a no-strings affair? She'd said she was too, but she'd been lying to herself and him. Had he been doing the same, or was she in this emotional quagmire on her own?

Dima led her back to the bedroom, starting to undress without even asking if she was ready for bed. But maybe her drooping eyes and frequent yawns had given her away.

While he seemed intent on being naked together, he made no effort to initiate sex, but pulled Jenna's body close to his before giving her a sweet and entirely chaste kiss good-night.

Considering how her mind was spinning, it should have been impossible for Jenna to sleep.

It wasn't.

For the first time ever, Jenna had no trouble sleeping on the plane. Of course, the fact she was doing it in an actual bed while snuggled closely to Dima's warm body could have something to do with it.

Dima woke her with a kiss. "You need to get up, *milaya moy*. We are landing momentarily. If you want a shower, now is the time to take it."

Feeling wonderfully rested, Jenna sat up. "I slept the whole trip?"

How could that be possible? Jenna never slept longer than nine hours, and that was only when she was full-on exhausted.

"You needed the rest."

"I bet you didn't sleep for twelve hours." She could not imagine it.

"No, but I enjoyed a full night's rest."

Full night for him, maybe.

She grimaced. "I won't sleep a wink tonight."

"I will not mind." The look he gave her said Dima had plans for their nighttime hours, and they didn't include a lot of sleeping regardless.

She laughed and shook her head. "I would ask if you think of anything else, but I know you do. I really enjoyed our time on the yacht."

"I did too, Jenna. You and I fit very well."

"Yes, we do."

His eyes widened in surprise, his body jerking in shock like her agreement had stunned him. Then he frowned. "Where real life does not intrude, you mean."

"I didn't say that."

But he was standing. "We touch down in thirty minutes." Then he left the bedroom.

What had just happened?

Jenna didn't know, but she didn't like feeling as if she was missing something elemental.

She did take a shower, though it was a quick one. She dressed appropriately for Abu Dhabi, her shoulders covered, and a casual scarf looped around her neck that could be used as a head covering if necessary.

Not that she thought they'd be going anywhere between the airport and the Merikov condo, but it was better to be prepared.

The royal condo was nothing like any condominium Jenna had ever seen. The seven-thousand-square-foot structure surrounded by palms and stone walls topped by decorative wrought-iron felt more like a stand-alone mansion than anything in a complex.

She said as much to Dima.

"We share a wall with two other smaller units used to house domestic and security staff." He shed his jacket and tie, hanging both over one arm. "The complex has its own security as well, which makes using the gym, private golf course and the like less problematic for residents."

It sounded like the perfect getaway spot for his royal family. "So what you are saying is that this very private complex offers additional security and amenities for the rich and famous."

"Yes." He frowned but seemed to shake off whatever was bothering him. "There is an Olympic-sized swimming pool that is fantastic for laps, but I prefer our private infinitely pool for relaxation."

"And other things, I bet," she teased, wanting the warm, bantering Dima from the evening before back.

This brooding alpha male was very sexy, but he made her feel sad, and she didn't know why.

"I've never brought another woman here." His tone implied he found the very thought obscene. "I don't bring lovers to my family's properties."

"I'm the exception?" Because she was definitely his lover.

"Can you doubt it?"

She didn't want to, especially now she had acknowledged the truth of her feelings for him, but she wasn't about to get into that. "One thing I don't doubt is that even if I'd gotten the deal of the century, I wouldn't be staying in accommodations nearly as nice as this."

The foyer opened to three different reception rooms through archways. One was a large living room, another a dining room that could easily accommodate sixteen if not twenty at the table. The other was a library that rivaled anything she'd ever seen in a private residence, even royal ones.

Beautiful furniture in dark wood graced each room, the upholstery different shades of the sunset. It was impressive and luxurious but didn't feel like a hotel.

"This reminds me of Piper Nikos's designs, but I thought she only did the properties her husband's company developed."

"You have a good eye. She did the decor when she was still running her private design firm."

"It's stood the test of time this long?" Jenna was impressed.

"There are six bedrooms, but we will only be using one of them."

"That library...this place doesn't feel like a property used for the occasional business meeting."

"It was my mother's favorite vacation spot."

And he'd brought Jenna to this clearly very private family oasis?

"You rarely mention her," she said softly, laying her hand on his arm.

Dima's handsome face showed old grief. "I was only a child when we lost her, but I still remember her smile."

"And that hurts?"

"Yes."

"Thank you."

He turned to face her. "For?"

"Not playing stoic he-man. Sharing your real emotions with me."

"According to you, I am no good at hiding them from you, regardless."

"I know you better than most people," she said consolingly.

He laughed. "Believe me when I tell you that my ego is not so fragile that your ability to read what most people do not bothers me."

He said that, but he'd brought up her ability to read him more than once.

It had to bother him at least a little.

She slid her hand down his arm to take his hand. "Let's explore."

The condo had a private media room. Unsurprising. And game room filled with board games from the antique to the latest offerings. Surprising. Six bedrooms, all with their own en suite bathrooms. Unsurprising. A small breakfast nook that opened onto a secluded outdoor garden with another eating area as well as a conversation grouping of cushioned outdoor furniture. A little surprising.

But the most surprising thing was how at home Jenna felt from the moment of crossing the condo's threshold. She could fit her own house into this condo several times over, and yet it felt warm and welcoming to her.

Or was that just the glow from realizing she was in love with the man she would be sleeping with that night?

Later, he took her on an evening kayak ride through the mangrove forest. It was amazing and magical, the smell of mangroves mixing with the scent of water teeming with wildlife and fauna. The sound of nightlife in the waterlogged forest was so not something she had expected to experience here.

When they landed back on the dock, Jenna was not at all surprised to discover he had dinner plans at one of the city's hottest restaurants.

They were shown to their table, and when she saw the mixed iris bouquet there, Jenna felt tears burn at the back of her eyes. "They're beautiful."

"Their recipient is even more beautiful."

"If I didn't know better, I would think you were woo-ing me, my prince." She leaned close to him, but not so close it would scandalize the other diners. "I'm a sure thing, Dima."

His even, white teeth flashed in a gorgeous smile, his gray eyes smoldering like molten metal. "As am I."

Dima seemed in an unusually good mood over dinner, and Jenna let herself relax and enjoy his company. She did not know what was coming, but she knew that right now, she was happy to be here, with this man.

As if by unspoken agreement, they were silent on the ride back to the condo.

When they got there, he made good on his promise to keep her awake late into the night, but it wasn't just mak-ing love. They played naked Parcheesi in the game room and snuck into the kitchen to make a snack in the wee hours of the morning before finally succumbing to sleep.

The next day, they both woke pretty early and enjoyed a leisurely swim in the infinity pool before breakfast. Con-trary to what she'd expected, Dima was happy to play in the water with her, without getting sexual.

Which made sense when the housekeeper came out to tell him he had a call.

They were surrounded by staff, even if that staff were adept at being unobtrusive. That phone call started Dima's workday, and Jenna decided to relax and read one of the books from her towering to-be-read stack.

Well, metaphorically. She'd brought her electronic reader with her, and it was loaded with the books she'd been too busy to read in the last year.

Jenna spent the next few hours taking turns reading in the sun, cooling off in the pool, and finally reading in the shade as the sun rose to its zenith.

Completely relaxed, she was startled when her phone rang with Emma's ringtone.

Grabbing it, Jenna found herself answering without any of the hesitation she'd been feeling the past couple of weeks. "Hi, Emma, what's up?"

"My husband does not think you betrayed his family's secrets."

"Okay, that's direct. What happened?"

"Kon admitted his attempt at matchmaking to me, and, well, we might be not speaking at the moment. The big, dumb prince didn't realize how hurt your feelings would be by the accusation."

"He didn't actually accuse me."

"Tell me you weren't hurt," Emma said, like she was daring Jenna to lie.

"I can't."

"And you still are, or you would have been answering my calls."

Jenna couldn't deny that either. "I answered now."

"Yes, you did. It makes me wonder what has changed. I was fully prepared to stalker-call you."

Jenna laughed at the reference to both Emma and Nataliya's habits of repeatedly calling when she didn't pick up right away. They didn't do it often, but both women could be a bit impatient about getting ahold of her when they felt they had something important to impart or discuss.

That laughter released something inside Jenna, and she realized she could and probably *should* talk to Emma about what had happened.

Nataliya was still off limits as a confidant, but once she'd passed her first trimester of pregnancy, the risk of miscarriage diminished considerably, and Jenna would be shocked if Nikolai didn't confess all to his wife.

Relieved she could talk this out with someone who

knew all the players well, Jenna told Emma the whole story. She finished off by telling her how she'd had to step back from doing what she believed to be right because of her relationship with the royal family.

"You probably wouldn't even have been a target for that deceitful B-I-T-Charlie if you weren't our friend."

Jenna had to smile at Emma's avoidance of using the term she made it clear she was thinking. "No, Skylar would have targeted me regardless. She was an equal opportunity thief of information. She must have thought she hit the mother lode with my contacts, though."

"Your brother's company is working on some very sensitive stuff."

"Exactly. It's a good thing we don't talk about his business much."

"Yes. Listen, Jenna, I'm sorry."

"Why are you sorry? You didn't accuse me of divulging sensitive information."

"Kon didn't either. Not really. He just wanted to get you and Dima together."

"Are you serious?" It was the second time Emma had made such a claim, so Jenna thought maybe she was, but it was so out there.

"Well, yes. I mean it was obvious to everyone you two had a thing for each other."

"My brother said the same."

"See?" Emma said like that settled it.

"We have a lot of chemistry," Jenna conceded.

"Oh, my gosh, are you admitting it? Nataliya owes me five bucks."

"You bet on it?"

"She bet me that you would never allow yourself to admit what you were feeling toward Dima because he's a prince."

"You took the bet?" Nataliya had been right, and Jenna hadn't actually ever planned to act on her overwhelming attraction to the youngest Merikov.

"Sure. I said that kind of sexual tension was going to explode sometime, and I bet it would happen before Prince Evengi's campaign to marry off his youngest son bore any fruit."

"Dima said he agreed to meet women his father introduced him to."

"I'm glad that doesn't bother you. You know it doesn't mean anything. Sometimes with my father-in-law, it's easier to just go along in the short run while holding out for your own plans in the long term."

"It sounds like you made five bucks on me. I think you owe me a coffee."

"But that's the whole profit."

Jenna laughed. Like the princess couldn't afford to buy her coffee. "Get my coffee money from Prince Konstantin. He owes me."

"That he does," Emma said with fervent agreement.

A week ago, Jenna would have been happy to keep rehashing everything, but she had bigger fish to fry now. "How do you handle it?"

"What? Having an arrogant husband who thinks he knows best?" Emma asked wryly.

Jenna laughed as she was meant to, but it was funny. Prince Konstantin had met his match in Emma, just as his kingly brother had in Nataliya. Neither woman was a pushover, and neither man would be happy if they were.

"Having people around all the time," Jenna explained her question. "Never being alone, even in your own home."

"I won't say it's not that bad. When you weren't raised to it like they were, it really is hard."

"And?"

"And you have to decide if it's worth it to you to change your life to be with someone who can't change theirs." Emma's words made it clear she knew this was about more than Jenna admitting she was attracted to Dima.

"You don't do all the compromising." Jenna had seen Emma put her foot down about things that were important to her.

"No, of course not. Kon really struggled at first with my insistence on what I call *family dinners* at least twice a week."

"But he works really hard to be there for dinner." Jenna had seen the prince in action, cutting off phone calls and taking meetings late so he could be there for dinner with his wife and two boys.

Nikolai and Nataliya did the same thing. Jenna had always assumed it was a family tradition, even for the Merikovs.

"You've probably noticed it is their family tradition, but for me family dinner means him and me cooking together in the kitchen, letting the boys help where they can and then sitting down to eat together as well."

"He didn't understand the need to cook together?" Jenna guessed.

"Exactly, but I wanted my children to understand that food doesn't magically come from the kitchen. Someone has to prepare it, and if you want to be self-sufficient, sometimes that someone needs to be you."

"Even if your father is a billionaire prince."

"Even then." Emma made a humming sound, like she was gathering her thoughts. "On family dinner nights, the staff are given time off."

"You all wash your own dishes?"

"Yes. Again, teaching our children that dishes and tables don't magically clean themselves."

"While giving your little family a couple of nights of privacy. Only you still have security."

"Not in the family quarters. Privacy is at a premium, I will not lie, but there are ways to prevent you from feeling like you live in a fishbowl."

"I'm pretty sure the media contributes to that feeling." The fear of scandal had played a major part in Jenna not being able to file charges against Skylar.

"Yes, but Mirrus is a small country, and the Merikovs aren't of nearly as much interest to the paparazzi as more well-known royals."

"They're of enough interest that news of Nataliya's miscarriage got leaked."

"Yes, and Dima got dumped in a very public manner, which the news cycle ran with," Emma agreed. "But honestly? I drop my children off at school like all the other parents, and there aren't a bunch of photographers hanging around, hoping to get a picture."

"Like every other parent with a security detail," Jenna teased.

"Sure, but I'm willing to live with that to know my children are safe, that my husband is safe. That I am safe."

"That's one thing I'll say for the Merikovs. They don't distinguish when it comes to security between the brothers."

"No. But they're all billionaires in their own right, because they each own one third of Mirrus Global."

"I don't think Prince Evengi would settle for anything less than the strongest security measures for any of them regardless." Jenna had seen how protective the sometimes interfering former king was toward his family.

"It's not really his call anymore, but I agree. Nikolai is pretty adamant."

"Tell me about it." There had been times over the past

years that Jenna had been assigned her own temporary security detail, and that was all down to Nikolai.

She'd dealt with the inconvenience for the sake of Nataliya's peace of mind and that of Jenna's own parents, who worried about her connection to a royal family. Jenna had also always known it was temporary.

The prospect of taking on that sort of thing permanently couldn't be dismissed just because she recognized the feelings she had for Dima.

However, neither could Jenna deny that she was more open to it than she had ever been before.

Love was a terribly powerful emotion. Her love for her brother Matt, and debilitating pain at losing him, had dictated choices in her life that might well impact her ability to have a long-term relationship with Dima.

CHAPTER THIRTEEN

JENNA WAS STILL mulling over her conversation with Emma when the scrape of sandals on the stone surround of the pool brought her head up.

Dima was dressed in chinos and a short-sleeved button-up. And yes, he was wearing sandals.

"Those aren't swim trunks," she said, a little stunned at this casually dressed Dima.

"No. I thought we could go to the Old Fort this afternoon."

She nodded, but her gaze was fixed on him, and her body wasn't moving.

"That hungry look in your eyes would make more sense if I *was* wearing swim trunks." His voice was laced with laughter.

"You mean European trunks, like swimmers wear?" she asked, her mind immediately going there and her tone husky from desire she made no attempt to hide.

"I believe I have a pair with me, yes."

He'd worn regular board shorts while swimming with her that morning.

Jenna fanned herself. "I'd like to see that."

"I'll change and join you," he said with alacrity.

"Yes." They could go to the museum tomorrow.

He was back in only a few minutes, wearing the promised swimsuit. The tight black fabric outlined his semi-erection and showcased his muscular thighs. Jenna sucked in air, trying to catch her breath.

Dima was hands down the sexiest man she had ever seen. Ever. Ever. Ever.

He dove into the water, coming up at the edge near where she sat under a shade tree. "Are you going to join me?"

She nodded, her mouth cotton-dry with anticipation. How did this man affect her so strongly, so quickly?

She dropped the gauzy swim wrap she'd been wearing to protect her skin from the sun.

His gray gaze remained steadily on her as she moved toward the pool and then sat down to slide in from the side. He was there before she even started sliding in, his body so close their skin touched as she let herself into the perfectly temperate water.

He pulled her in to him. "The thought of you out here in nothing but your bikini has been driving me mad all day."

"I was just reading, and swimming. Nothing exciting."

"You are exciting." He kissed her with a passion that gave truth to his words.

She responded, her entire body straining toward him in primal response.

His hands got busy at the back of her bikini top while he deepened the kiss. The thought of baring her breasts to him sent thrills through her and then chills.

Breaking her mouth from his, Jenna pressed against his chest. "You can't do that! Someone will see."

"We are alone."

"But what about the staff? Security?" The very people she was trying to decide if she could live with on a daily basis.

"I sent them to their condos."

"We're really alone?"

"The alarm system is armed, and all the cameras are monitored."

"Is there a camera back here?"

"There is, but I told them to turn it off until dark. There is no approach to the condo that is not monitored. They do not need to watch us now."

"You're sure?"

"I promise you, *milaya moy*. We are entirely private here."

"In that case…" She dove back into the kiss.

He peeled away her bikini and threw the top onto the stone surround. Then he cupped her breasts, brushing his thumbs over her nipples.

She shivered against him, running her hands up his back, loving the feel of his rippling muscles under her fingers. It excited her that he'd changed his plans so easily when she showed interest in him.

Being wanted like that was heady.

One of his hands slid down her back and into her bikini bottoms until his blunt fingertip pressed against her entrance. He traced her labia, sending sensation pulsing through her core.

She ran her hands along his backside, squeezing tight muscles and making him groan. But she wanted something more, needed to touch another part of him.

Jenna brought her hands between them to caress his length. He pressed into her hands with another pleasure-filled groan.

Jenna tugged his hard-on out of its Lycra confines. It was hot and big, bobbing in the water, even as she curled her fingers around it.

Her fingertips didn't quite meet, but she used both hands to compensate as she'd learned to do in her short time as his lover. They touched each other, building the pleasure between them until the need to join was pulsing through her.

But it was Dima who broke the kiss this time to say, "I need to be in you, now."

"Yes."

She shoved her bikini bottoms down her legs and kicked them off, not caring where they went. Then she hopped up, spreading her legs so her thighs were on either side of him, and she crossed her ankles.

The head of his erection brushed her opening, and they both shuddered.

Desire was pulsating through her, but so was emotion. Jenna felt connected to Dima like she'd never been to anyone else. She'd spent years keeping people, even Nataliya, at a certain distance.

And somehow this prince had made it past barriers forged in the pain of loss and fear of her own body's genetics.

She needed him inside her, but even just being held like this, their connection reached to the core of her soul and held on tight.

Jenna used the water to shift easily as she settled over his erection, explosions of ecstasy going off inside her as she lowered herself onto him.

"Yes, just like that, *milaya moy.*" Dima held on to her hips with both hands, helping her to stay close even as they began to move.

The water made her buoyant, but it also increased the friction, not as silky smooth as her own natural wetness. It all added to the moment, and they strained together, chasing that pinnacle of pleasure. He came first, his shout loud and his body going rigid.

The way he swelled inside her as he came was the final stimulation she needed to go over, and Jenna cried out as she climaxed too.

The water moved them together, causing pleasant aftershocks until Jenna let her head fall forward to rest against his neck.

"You did say you wanted to work me out of your system," she said, teasing. Mostly.

Part of her wanted him to deny it.

What he said was, "I'm not sure that will ever be possible, but we can keep trying."

He sounded like he was teasing too, but right then Jenna could not be sure. It was the worst time for her ability to read him to go on the fritz.

The pang in her heart needed him to be joking.

If he was still intent on sexing her out of his system, Jenna was in for a world of hurt. But then, she'd never acknowledged things had changed for her either.

She wasn't sure that either of them had the courage it took for complete emotional honesty, but at least when they were making love, they both offered nothing but raw truth and their need-tinged ecstasy.

Dimitri lay awake, Jenna held close to his body.

She had a list of reasons why marriage between them would not work. He was a prince and active member of a royal family. If she would just admit it, she would see that she too was an active member of a royal family and had been since Nataliya agreed to marry Nikolai.

His status as a billionaire who required staff and security would be a plus to a lot of women, and men, but for his Jenna? Not so much.

He was five years younger, and that could not be changed, but it was hardly the barrier she thought it was. Jenna was the woman he wanted at his side, and he did not care that she was thirty-five, rather than twenty-five and primed to have children.

Her self-imposed sterility was something he admired, because it showed how much she was willing to give up to protect future generations. How could he feel anything but respect at that? It was certainly no reason for them not to marry. If they decided they wanted children, there were options.

How could she not see how perfectly they fit together? Not only in the bedroom, but outside of it.

She'd been hurt when he'd had to stop her pressing charges against Skylar, but he thought Jenna had come to terms with that.

He was damn lucky, and he knew it. Looking back, he'd messed up on a huge scale with the timing of their first time making love too, but again…she'd forgiven him.

Now, he just had to show her that he was more than his title. That he was a man capable of enhancing her life, not only making it more difficult.

There was nothing he could change about most of her reservations about a future with him, other than show her that they were not the barrier she believed them to be. Except for one thing.

And he had to think long and hard how much he was willing to give up to be with the woman he had decided was perfect for him. But if he took the step he was considering, it could well wash away her concerns about her sterility as well.

He had just under two weeks to show her that all her misgivings were about things that were not as important as how much they needed each other.

And she did need him. Just as he needed her.

Jenna's phone range, interrupting her doze beside the pool. She pulled it up and noted it was a video call. From Nataliya.

She swiped to answer immediately.

"When were you going to tell me you were dating my youngest brother-in-law?" Nataliya demanded as soon as the call connected.

Jenna was in too good a mood to even work up some worry about discussing this with her BFF. "There wasn't any chance of me dating the other one," she teased rather than answering.

Nataliya's lovely face twisted in distaste. "No kidding. Even if the guy wasn't so gone on Emma, you two would have murdered each other in your sleep if you tried to actually sleep together."

Still not completely over Prince Konstantin's matchmaking methods, Jenna could only agree. "Yep."

"So, you and Dima?"

"He's kind of perfect for me."

"Even though he's a prince with a pretty high-handed way of handling life?" Nataliya didn't pull any punches.

"No one is perfect." Jenna shifted in her lounge chair and pulled her wrap on, using the new portable phone stand Dima had gotten her without compunction.

She was carrying a purse again too. It helped that he'd asked his security team to go through all the stuff she'd brought with her one last time to set her mind at ease.

Relaxed in the certainty no one was spying on her, Jenna was thoroughly enjoying her holiday.

"No," Nataliya said with alacrity. "Though Dima is a good guy, even if he isn't perfect."

"He really is." One of the best actually.

"You know, I was sure you'd never give in to your feelings for him." Nataliya peered at her phone screen like she was trying to look inside Jenna's head.

Jenna just shrugged. "He can be very persuasive."

"In other words, you could fight your own needs, but not his too."

"You're so wise, oh, pregnant one."

Nataliya grimaced. "I'm so nauseated, it's ridiculous, but my doctor assures me that's a good sign."

"Can they give you anything for it?"

"Stop worrying about me. I'll be fine. Women have been dealing with pregnancy nausea throughout history."

"Yes, but—"

"Don't. The miscarriage was an anomaly, and there's no reason to suspect it will happen again, but if it does? I know you'll be there for me, just like last time."

Jenna nodded fast.

Nataliya's brown eyes warmed with compassion. "You never talk about it."

"About what?"

"Your sterility."

No point in talking about what could not be changed. "It was my choice."

"But that doesn't mean you never wanted to be a mom." Nataliya bit her lip, her gaze sheening over. "I never asked. I'm sorry."

"Oh, no, pregnancy hormones are making you maudlin."

"Don't joke. I'm a bad friend."

"You're the best of friends, and you're right, there's a part of me that will always grieve not having children. I know some people are just as happy not to have them, and my life is full, but being an aunt gives me more joy than just about anything."

"Like Dima?"

"Like Dima."

Nataliya put her hand over her heart and fake swooned. "You admit it?"

"I'm vacationing with him. I wouldn't think much of

my own decision-making skills if I were doing that and didn't find happiness in his company."

Nataliya's eyes widened, and she gasped. "You're in love with him!"

"No comment."

Suddenly her royal bestie went all serious compassion. "Are you going to let yourself be with him?"

"I am with him." What did Nataliya think, they had separate bedrooms?

"You know what I mean."

And just that quickly, Jenna did. "We went into this saying no strings. Neither of us has verbalized a change to that status quo. Well, other than to promise fidelity as long as we are together."

"I'd say that was a commitment."

Jenna shrugged. "It is and it isn't."

"Do you want a future with Dima?"

"We're really compatible," Jenna hedged.

"That's not an answer."

"I don't know. I think I do, but everything here is so idyllic."

Jenna spent her mornings by the pool, swimming, reading and catching up on her shows on her phone. Then Dima joined her either before or after lunch, and they spent the rest of the day and evening together.

They'd gone to the Old Fort, shopping and dining on the waterfront. Yesterday, he'd surprised her by not going to work after their morning swim and breakfast. He'd taken her to Yas, a small, exclusive island off the coast, where they'd spent the whole day in a private cabana, enjoying the sun, the sand and the water.

They had plans to visit the Grand Mosque later that day.

But none of this was real life.

"Vacation isn't real life," Nataliya said, like she was reading Jenna's mind.

Considering how close they were, it wasn't a stretch.

"No, it's not," Jenna agreed.

Nataliya nodded, like she'd made up her mind about something. "Do you remember what you told me when I thought Nikolai was too good to be true?"

"To tap that?" Jenna joked.

Nataliya's laugh and the joy on her BFF's face warmed Jenna's heart.

"Something like that. You definitely said go for it."

"But you knew Nikolai wanted to marry you."

"What do you know about Dima?"

"He wants my body. A lot."

Nataliya rolled her eyes. "We *all* know that. What do *you* know?"

"He's ruthless, but he cares about my feelings. He's arrogant, but he's not impossible to reason with."

"Sounds like Dima."

"You two have been friends a long time."

"We have, but Jenna, I've never been his lover."

The light went on. "I know he's vulnerable in ways he'll never show. I know that his time in the military changed him. I know that protecting his family is paramount, but he considers me part of that family."

"Now we're getting somewhere."

She knew that he wanted sex without barriers between them and had taken that step with her when he had not done so with any other lover, but that was too private to share, even with Nataliya.

"I know he doesn't think any of the obstacles I see to us being together are insurmountable." And that was why he hadn't belabored them.

Because Dima had not seen any of her concerns as

things that could not be addressed. Though how he thought to get past her aversion to being part of a royal family in actual fact, she did not know.

"I know he took time off to spend with me here, when he never takes time off." She smiled at that knowledge.

"You're going to have to negotiate yearly vacations, or you won't get them," Nataliya warned.

"He *is* a workaholic. He's a prince and he's a billionaire, but that's not all he is."

"Isn't it?" Nataliya goaded, maybe because she'd said something similar a time or two about her own husband to Jenna.

"No. He's funny and educated, and he is always learning new things. He can be harsh, but he can be really compassionate too. He loves his nieces and nephews."

"So do you."

"I do." How Jenna had even entertained for a minute, much less a couple of days, the idea that she could cut ties with this family, she did not know.

They were as much Jenna's people as Luke, Lisa and her family and their parents.

"I love you, Nataliya."

"I love you too, friend. You're my sister in all the ways that matter. I won't lie and say making that official wouldn't thrill me to bits."

"You're getting ahead of yourself," Jenna warned. "I haven't said anything about marriage." But she was thinking it.

"Maybe you should." Nataliya's words hung there between them for several silent seconds.

Finally, Jenna asked, "What?"

"Maybe *you* should propose to Dima."

Jenna felt her lungs seize, and then she gasped, her lungs filling again. "You're not serious."

"Why not?" Nataliya got a mischievous look on her face. "I'll leave you to chew on that. I need to go eat some soda crackers, or I'm going to puke."

Jenna was still pondering that *Why not?* as she dressed for lunch. Dima was supposed to be done with his video conference calls in time to join her.

She'd donned a flowy nineties retro dress with wedge sandals and chunky jewelry. Her blond hair hung loose around her shoulders, silky and smooth from her trip to the salon after her phone call with Nataliya.

Dima had told her to dress nice because they were going someplace special for dinner.

So far, everything they'd done had been special.

She couldn't find the scarf she'd brought to wear with this dress, so she pulled her case out to see if it had gotten left inside.

"You are not leaving me over this!" Dima's cold, autocratic tone had her spinning around to face him.

His expression closed, he stood in the doorway, a brooding and physical barrier.

"I'm not leaving." But what did he mean by *this*?

"You're packing."

"Um, no. I'm looking for my scarf. Why would I be packing?" Jenna finally focused on the tabloid in his hand.

From where she stood, she could see a picture of her and Dima while they walked along the Corniche. "We knew word would get out. We've hardly been discreet about this vacation."

He'd held her hand wherever they went, when it was acceptable to do so. They arrived and departed in the same car. They'd made no effort to obfuscate her presence in his family's home.

More to the point, why would she leave Abu Dhabi just because the inevitable had happened?

"I have no desire to hide that we are dating," he assured her, though his tone said anything but.

She nodded, agreeing. "So what has you so upset?"

"I am not upset."

"Okay." Honestly? He didn't look so much upset as, well, angry. "Are you mad about something?"

"I thought you were leaving." He glared at her suitcase.

Why would he think that? Even if she had her case out? "Because the media picked up on the fact we're dating? I'm not that thin-skinned."

Besides, the only people she worried about finding out already knew. And they didn't care. Not her family. Not his.

Nataliya had been sending Jenna teasing texts about Dima, and humorous memes about morning sickness, ever since they got off the phone.

"We're not just dating," he said firmly. "We are lovers."

That would feel more romantic if he had said it with a smidge more emotion and less chilly factualism.

"True." She reached for the paper. Something in the article had to be the reason he was acting like this. "Here, let me see."

He held tight to the newspaper. "If you haven't seen it, you don't need to."

Was he kidding? "That's not how it works, Dima. Not for me, anyway."

"You said you understood."

"What did I say I understood?"

"Me seeing the women my father picked out for me. You knew it wasn't going anywhere." He spoke dismissively, like it was a nonissue.

Only she didn't know what the issue was, and now she wanted to, badly.

"That's what you said." She couldn't pretend to be thrilled his father was looking elsewhere for a bride for Dima, though.

However, the older man had no idea that the relationship between Jenna and Dima had changed. So the only people they could blame for Prince Evengi's attempts at matchmaking were themselves.

"It is what I said, and I expect you to trust me," Dima assured her, all arrogance.

That trust thing was still a bit of a sticking point, and Jenna never reacted well to being told what she was supposed to do, much less feel.

"Let me see," she said again, this time her own tone matching his more closely.

"Fine, if you insist." He handed the paper over, but even under all that chill, she could read his reluctance to do so. "We made the front cover."

His disdain for that reality dripped from his voice. Then, without another word, he spun on his heel and walked from the room.

For a moment, staring at the empty room where he'd just been, Jenna forgot the tabloid. Didn't he care how she reacted to whatever it was that had him acting so strangely? Wasn't she important enough for him to stick around and have it out, whatever *it* was?

Uncertainty filled her, feeding her fears that despite her change of heart, they had no real future. Her prince did not care if she was upset by what she was about to read.

If he did, he would have stuck around. Wouldn't he?

Only, the first thing he'd said was, *You're not leaving me.* Not, *You're not leaving Abu Dhabi.* Was that because

Dima was a possessive alpha male who expected everyone around him to fall into his plans?

Or because *she* mattered to *him*? Jenna knew what she needed to be true, but she was a mature woman, who could and would accept the *real* truth, whatever it was.

Even if it meant coming to terms with a prince who was seeing his father's matchmaking candidates because Dima saw those women as better potential life partners than her.

She lifted the paper and focused on the front cover.

It was a European tabloid, so that they were featured on the front cover was kind of surprising. Until Jenna saw the rest of the front-page splash.

Prince Dimitri Already Cheating on Princess Sophia!

Two pictures were side by side on the cover with a diagonal split. In one, Dima danced with a beautiful twentysomething woman wearing a formal gown. The background was familiar to Jenna. It was in the grand ballroom at the palace in Mirrus.

Dima and Princess Sophia were both smiling and looking into each other's eyes.

The other photo showed Jenna and Dima walking hand in hand along the waterfront, as she'd noted. What she hadn't been able to see from across the room was their expressions.

Jenna was looking out over the water, a half smile on her face. Dima was looking at her, his expression intent. If she could believe what her eyes were telling her, there was a wealth of emotion in that intent gaze too.

Jenna flipped open the scandal rag and found the article. Speculation had been rife since Dima's latest trip to

Mirrus, when he had singled Princess Sophia out at a formal function to dance and chat with.

There were several pictures of them together, but Jenna gave those photos nothing more than a glance. It was the pictures of her and Dima that caught her attention and would not let go.

They looked like two people in love. While the paper painted her as *the other woman* in a nonexistent love triangle, their photographer had captured the truth. Dima looked at her like he looked at no one else.

Jenna wasn't immune either. She had a particularly besotted expression in one of the shots, but her affection for him shone through in all of the pictures, if you knew what to look for.

Had Dima seen her love for him? Was that what really had him riled?

Only, again…he'd told her she wasn't leaving him. And he'd said it in that ruthless way that he usually reserved for business. He'd meant it.

Could it really simply be about sex for him?

The pictures said otherwise, because if they showed Jenna's love, they were equally revealing about an amount of emotion coming from Dima that did not jibe with their relationship being nothing more than friendship and sex.

He'd been adamant when he said they were lovers, and she couldn't help wondering…hoping…that meant they were two people in love as well as sexual partners.

The only way to find out the truth would be to talk to him. One thing Jenna knew. She wasn't walking away from this thing with Dima without having a real conversation about real feelings.

She found him sitting sideways on a lounger by the pool, his head bent, his focus on the empty, sparkling water, a whiskey in his hand.

It was a Dima as she had never seen him. His tie was askew, the top button undone on his shirt. His jacket had been discarded entirely, and his hair looked like he'd been in a windstorm. Or, you know, running his fingers through it and tugging at it in agitation.

So not like Dima.

"I'd like the originals." She stopped beside him, letting her knee bump his leg. "Do you think we could get them?"

He looked up, his expression grim. "They're already online. Even I can't put that genie back in the box."

Suddenly far more sure of herself than she had been in the bedroom, Jenna smiled. "Even you?"

His bleak expression didn't lighten.

Jenna shook her head. "Have a look at those pictures, Dima."

"I have looked."

"Then you know they answer a question I've been asking myself since we got to Abu Dhabi."

"What question?"

"Set yourself to rights and I'll tell you over dinner."

"We were to go to the Grand Mosque first."

"Then let's go to the Grand Mosque," she agreed easily.

"That's why you were looking for your scarf."

"Yes. It would not be appropriate to enter the mosque without a head covering."

He stood up, but arrogant, autocratic Dima was gone. Her prince looked like he didn't know what to do with himself.

Jenna stepped right up into his space and leaned up to kiss the underside of his jaw. "Go take a shower. You'll feel better for it."

"Join me."

"If I do, we won't leave the condo, and I have plans for tonight."

"I did too. Have plans for tonight."

"Well, then…" She indicated the bathroom with a tilt of her chin.

CHAPTER FOURTEEN

Jenna finished reading the article while Dima was in the shower.

The sheer amount of lies and speculation might have staggered her if she hadn't been Nataliya's BFF.

But Jenna had been best friends since university to a lady who lived like a normal person, who married and became a princess and then, finally a queen.

This article was no worse than most and better than some. Yes, they implied Dima and the princess had some kind of family merger deal, like the contract Nataliya had signed so many years ago. They had even dug up old dirt on Prince Konstantin, during the years when he'd had a lot of one-night stands. Comparisons were implied. Dirt was slung, but really?

It wasn't the end of the world.

Not for her. Not for Dima.

By tacit agreement, they did not discuss the article while they visited the Grand Mosque. Neither did they dwell on it while driving through the city.

The special dinner he'd had planned later was at the end of a pretty long drive into the desert. A large Turkish rug had been laid out for a picnic on the sand.

Flaming torches positioned around it cast a soft golden glow over the piled pillows and delicious-smelling dishes arranged in the center on a low table. The stars and moon glowed in the night sky like they never did in the city.

"This is amazing, Dima. Thank you for setting this up."

"You said you wanted to come into the desert. I was going to take you on a Bedouin experience, but realized I wanted privacy more."

"I love it." She kicked off her sandals and found a seat among the plump cushions.

After removing his own shoes, Dima joined her.

"I know the security people and whoever set this up are around, but it feels so private out here."

"After securing the perimeter, they have all gone to the other side of that dune." Dima sounded very satisfied by that and proud of himself. "If we are loud, our sounds will carry, but other than that, we are effectively alone."

"You think we are going to do something that could make us loud?" she teased, but the reminder that sex was his primary reason for being with her reared its ugly head again.

He gave her a look. "That was the plan, before I found you packing."

"I wasn't packing."

"I thought you were."

Jenna laid her hand over his. "Don't you know? I'm too stubborn and vocal to just take off without shouting it out first?"

"Shouting?"

"If I'm angry enough to leave you, there will be shouting."

"You read the article."

"I did."

"You do not seem angry."

"Well, I know the truth."

"You do?"

She nearly rolled her eyes but realized this was too serious to downplay in any way. "Yes, I do. If you want me to trust you, Dima, you have to trust me as well."

"I do trust you."

"Then trust me when I say that no tabloid article is going to make me question the truth that I know."

"What truth is that?" he asked, sounding cautious.

She'd get there, but they were doing some talking first.

"Don't you think it's funny that it never even occurred to that tabloid journalist that you are wooing me?" she asked, rather than answering.

Wooing was such an old-fashioned term, but it fit. He *had* been courting her.

"Lack of imagination and foresight," Dima said with a shrug in his tone.

She smiled up at him. "You don't deny that you've been courting me."

"Why would I deny the truth?"

"I don't know. Why tell me you were just trying to get me out of your system?"

Even in the muted light cast by the torches, she could see the color that burnished his chiseled features. "You did not want to hear the truth."

"You might be right."

"But now you claim to know it."

"Oh, I know all right. Have you looked at those photos?"

"The ones in the tabloid?" he asked, his dark brows furrowed.

"Yes."

"For a moment."

"You should have looked longer."

"Why?"

"They show the truth of the situation, no matter what lascivious lies the reporter claims."

"They show that I am wholly into you and not inter-ested in other women, regardless of their status," he said skeptically.

"Yes."

Clearly startled, he asked, "They do?"

"Why do you think I wanted the originals?"

"To destroy them."

"Not on your life. They're going in an album along with all the other snaps I've taken since we arrived in the UAE."

"You're a strange woman, Jenna."

"Maybe, but you like me this way." Those pictures had given her a confidence she had not felt until seeing them, and she was beginning to believe it was a certainty of her place in his life that could never again be taken away.

"I do."

"Why?" she asked.

"Because you are smart and lovely. I can't keep my hands off you, but I enjoy every moment I spend with you in and out of the bedroom."

"I meant why do you want to marry me?" Though his list of reasons why he liked her was very nice.

"Who said I did?"

"You, with your wooing."

"I think it's just called *dating* in this century."

"No."

"No?"

"No. Dating can be casual. You even tried to pretend it *was* casual, but there's nothing casual about how we feel about each other."

"Admitting we're not casual is as good as you calling me *your* prince," he said with satisfaction.

"I do that?"

"You have, on very rare occasions."

"I do think of you as mine."

His expression was growing more and more deliciously predatory. "The possessiveness is entirely mutual."

"Good to know."

"We fit. Even though I am a billionaire prince who cannot take a full vacation, we fit."

"Even though I cannot give you children?" she asked, old pain as close to the surface as it had ever been.

"If we want children, we can adopt, or use a surrogate. Or if you want the experience of carrying my child, we can use IVF with your sister's egg, or, if she does not want to do that, with eggs donated to a fertility clinic."

"You've thought a lot about this," she said faintly, finding it hard to get a breath to speak. "Really a lot."

"Naturally. I do not have to have children for the line. You need to accept that my place in the family means any children we might have would not carry high nobility titles, but if you want it, I would love to be a father."

Tears burned Jenna's eyes. "You would make a really good father."

"I like to think so. You would be an ideal mother. Strong and a great role model for both our sons and daughters."

"You sound like you want a lot of children. You do realize I'm thirty-five."

"Women are having children later in life, but if you do not want to do that, it is not a deal breaker for me."

"You would not resent me if I never wanted children at all?"

"No. *Milaya moy*, I want *you*. I think I need you."

She nodded to herself. "Are you afraid of the *L*-word?"

"I…" He tugged at the collar of his silk dress shirt, his expression guarded. "I thought love was off the table."

"Did you?" He had a rude awakening coming then.

"I thought you were perfect for me. I didn't need to consider beyond that."

That's what he thought. Jenna did not agree, even a little. The *L*-word would be spoken.

"I was perfect for you even if you did have a list of things you thought were wrong with me," he added.

"Not you, your role as a prince."

"I can give that up," he said as casually as he might tell her the time. Only that was not a casual statement. Not at all. "I cannot change the billionaire thing, or that I am my father's son, but I can abdicate my role as prince."

Jenna felt like all the air had been squeezed out of her surroundings, which of course was impossible. But had he just offered to repudiate his role as a prince in the House of Merikov?

"You don't mean that."

"I do. I spoke to my brother Nikolai. It is not without precedence. Other Merikovs have chosen the life of a commoner over that of royalty."

"I would like to hear those stories."

"Ask my father. He loves to expound on family history."

"You *do* love me."

"I must, because I have always been very proud to be a Prince of Mirrus."

"I would never ask you to give that up." Jenna shifted so she was on her knees in front of Dima. She reached out and took his hand.

His usually confident expression bemused, he let her.

She started to speak, but found she had to clear her suddenly dry throat. "I love you, and don't think I'll ever let you forget I said it first."

"I am sure my words tonight have been infused with my love for you. What are three little words in the face of all I will do to bring you happiness?"

"Those three little words *are* happiness, Dima." He should never doubt how important they were.

"Then I shall say them."

"There you go being all formal again."

"It happens when I am feeling nervous."

"Good to know."

"As if you need anything else in the way of telling my secrets."

She didn't reply, just waited, because her prince was no coward.

"I love you, Jenna mine. I do not care about the age difference, or your sterility, or how different our lives are. I need you to complete my life."

"I need you to complete mine." Sure, Jenna could live the rest of her life without Dima, but it would not be as rich, as full, as it would be *with* him. "Will you marry me, Dima?"

He went utterly still, and then the most beautiful smile broke over his gorgeous features. "I suppose you will never let me forget you asked first either?"

"I'm telling our children this story every year on our anniversary."

He pulled her up and against him, his mouth hovering a breath away from hers. "Yes, *milaya moy*. I will marry you."

They kissed to seal the deal, and that kiss held something none of theirs had before, a certainty of each other. It was like adding cinnamon to coffee, making the kiss better than any they had shared.

"Just tell your brother that I don't want to be a princess," she instructed when they were settled against the cushions, arms wrapped around each other.

"I can tell him, but unless I abdicate my role, I cannot stop him bestowing the honor on you."

"If he does it, I'll start lobbying for a constitutional monarchy."

"You will do that anyway."

Joy bubbling like champagne inside her, she laughed. "I will."

The kiss that followed was incendiary. Soon, they were making love and doing their best not to be overheard, but ultimately, Jenna couldn't care less who knew she and her prince had just promised each other a lifetime.

EPILOGUE

SIX MONTHS AFTER they'd eloped, Jenna patted her barely protruding tummy and smiled to herself.

It had taken only one round of IVF, since her uterus was entirely viable, for her to get pregnant with Dima's baby. Having a tubal ligation had not impacted her other otherwise healthy reproductive system. They had decided to use donated eggs from a donor who shared Jenna's physical characteristics, but not her genes.

The donors at the clinic were all screened for genetic diseases, and Jenna could be confident she wasn't passing anything on to the next generation that would devastate a family like hers had been.

It still felt like a miracle.

She'd never thought to be pregnant, and she wasn't sure she wanted to carry another child.

This one had come with aching pain in her back and hips as well as nausea every day, all day long for the first four months. She had finally stopped throwing up, and now she could be around her BFF again, who was pregnant with her fourth child.

Nataliya had given birth to a healthy baby a couple of months before Dima and Jenna decided that they would elope rather than deal with the rigmarole of a royal wedding. Jenna knew it was more for her sake than his and loved him for it.

Nataliya's fourth pregnancy had come as a shock to everyone. Their baby was only a few months old, but other than the nausea, Nataliya's pregnancy was progressing fine.

Unfortunately, she and Jenna had set each other off with their nausea and had to settle for texts for weeks.

Now they were getting together on Mirrus to celebrate Prince Evengi's birthday.

The former king was delighted all of his sons were happily married, but even more happy with his own lovely wife. Nataliya's mother had blossomed here on Mirrus, and Jenna loved seeing that.

She remembered the woman from when Jenna and Nataliya had first become friends. There had always been a sad look in Princess Solomia's eyes when she thought her daughter wasn't looking.

That sadness was gone. Being a grandmother suited the woman to the bone, and had done since the birth of Anna Yelena. Being married to her own arrogant prince had done wonders as well.

Nikolai and Nataliya were still sickeningly in love and the happy proud parents of three children, with a fourth on the way. Nataliya had finally determined four might be enough.

Emma and Konstantin were here with their boys for the birthday celebration as well. Jenna and Konstantin had finally made up, after sufficient groveling on the prince's part.

Konstantin's idea of matchmaking left a lot to be desired and she'd told him so.

Strong arms slid around her from behind, Dima's hands coming to rest against her stomach. "How is she doing today?"

"Active. Can you feel her?"

The baby kicked, and Dima made a sound of wonder as he always did. "I can. To think in only a few months' time we will be able to hold her."

"Can you believe Nataliya is having her fourth baby?"

"I can, but I admit I like our plan of adopting our next child."

"I do too." Jenna had this deep feeling that they were supposed to adopt their next child, and not a baby.

Dima had been all for it.

"We have a good life, Jenna."

"The best," she agreed with a happy hum.

"My brother is doing another study on the feasibility of shifting to a constitutional monarchy."

Jenna spun in her husband's arms. "Are you serious?"

He smiled down at her. "How can you doubt it? You, Nataliya and Emma make very persuasive advocates."

"Oh, I'm so happy."

"There is no guarantee he will shift our government in that direction."

"Nikolai is a good and fair man. Once he sees it will help and not hurt Mirrus, he will go for it."

"I love your confidence."

"I love you."

"Never stop saying that."

"I won't. Even if I did…"

"Have to say it first," he finished for her and then kissed her.

Love flowed around them as their mouths joined, as it always did. Her prince loved her with his whole great heart, and she loved him the same.

Even if it *was* his fault she had been bestowed with the title of Princess.

* * * * *

If you loved this thrilling finale to
Lucy Monroe's Princesses by Decree trilogy
make sure to check out the first two books,
available now!

His Majesty's Hidden Heir
Queen by Royal Appointment

WE HOPE YOU ENJOYED
THIS BOOK FROM

H HARLEQUIN

PRESENTS

Escape to exotic locations where passion knows no bounds.

Welcome to the glamorous lives of royals and billionaires, where passion knows no bounds. Be swept into a world of luxury, wealth and exotic locations.

8 NEW BOOKS AVAILABLE EVERY MONTH!

#3993 PENNILESS AND PREGNANT IN PARADISE
Jet-Set Billionaires
by Sharon Kendrick
One extraordinary Balinese night in the arms of guarded billionaire Santiago shakes up Kitty's life forever! She'll confess she's pregnant, but she'll need more than their scorching chemistry to accept his convenient proposal!

#3994 THE ROYAL BABY HE MUST CLAIM
Jet-Set Billionaires
by Jadesola James
When a scandalous night results in a shock baby, Princess Kemi ends up wearing tycoon Luke's ring! She fears she's swapping gilded cages as she struggles to break into his impenetrable heart. But will their Seychelles honeymoon set her free?

#3995 INNOCENT IN THE SICILIAN'S PALAZZO
Jet-Set Billionaires
by Kim Lawrence
Soren Steinsson-Vitale knows Anna Randall is totally off-limits. She's his sworn enemy's granddaughter and he's also her boss. But one kiss promises a wild connection that will lead them straight to his palazzo bedroom!

#3996 REVEALING HER NINE-MONTH SECRET
Jet-Set Billionaires
by Natalie Anderson
After one magical evening ended in disaster, Carrie assumed she'd never see superrich Massimo again. So, a glimpse of him nine months later sends her into labor—with the secret she didn't know she was carrying!

HPCNMRA0222

#3997 CINDERELLA FOR THE MIAMI PLAYBOY
Jet-Set Billionaires
by Dani Collins

Bianca Palmer's world hasn't been the same since going into hiding and becoming a housekeeper. So, she's shocked to discover her boss is Everett Drake—the man she shared a mesmerizing encounter with six months ago! And their attraction is just as untamable...

#3998 THEIR ONE-NIGHT RIO REUNION
Jet-Set Billionaires
by Abby Green

When Ana conveniently wed tycoon Caio, they were clear on the terms: one year to expand his empire and secure her freedom. But as the ink dries on their divorce papers, they're forced together for twenty-four hours...and an unrealized passion threatens to combust!

#3999 SNOWBOUND WITH HIS FORBIDDEN PRINCESS
Jet-Set Billionaires
by Pippa Roscoe

Princess Freya is dreading facing Kjell Bergqvist again. He's nothing like the man who broke her heart eight years ago. But memories of what they once shared enflame new desires when a snowstorm leaves them scandalously, irresistibly stranded...

#4000 RETURN OF THE OUTBACK BILLIONAIRE
Jet-Set Billionaires
by Kelly Hunter

Seven years ago, Judah Blake took the fall for a crime he didn't commit to save Bridie Starr. Now his family's land is in *her* hands, and to reclaim his slice of the Australian outback, he'll claim her!

YOU CAN FIND MORE INFORMATION ON UPCOMING HARLEQUIN TITLES, FREE EXCERPTS AND MORE AT HARLEQUIN.COM.

HPCNMRB0222

She needed him to turn. Would she see those disturbingly green
eyes? Would she see a sensual mouth? If he stepped closer would
she hear a voice that whispered wicked invitation and willful
temptation? All those months ago she'd been so seduced by him
she'd abandoned all caution, all reticence for a single night of
silken ecstasy only to then—

A sharp pain lanced, shocking her back to the present. Winded,
she pressed her hand to her stomach. How the mind could wreak
havoc on the body. The stabbing sensation was a visceral reminder
of the desolate emptiness she'd been trying to ignore for so long.

She'd recovered from that heartbreak. She was living her best
life here—free and adventurous, bathing in the warm, brilliant
waters of the Pacific. Her confusion was because she was tired.
But she couldn't resist stepping closer—even as another sharp pain
stole her breath.

"That's interesting." He addressed the man beside him. "Why
are—"

Shock deadened her senses, muting both him and the pain still
squeezing her to the point where she couldn't breathe. That *voice*?
That low tone that invited such confidence and tempted the listener
to share their deepest secrets?

Massimo hadn't just spoken to her. He'd offered the sort of attention that simply stupefied her mind and left her able only to say *yes*. And she had. Like all the women who'd come before her. And doubtless all those after.

Now his brief laugh was deep and infectious. Despite her distance, it was as if he had his head intimately close to hers, his arm around her waist, his lips brushing her highly sensitized skin—

Pain tore through her muscles, forcing her to the present again. She gasped as it seared from her insides and radiated out with increasingly harsh intensity. She stared, helpless to the power of it as that dark head turned in her direction. His green-eyed gaze arrowed on her.

Massimo.

"Carrie?" Sereana materialized, blocking him from her view. "Are you okay?" Her boss looked as alarmed as she sounded.

Carrie crumpled as the cramp intensified. It was as if she'd been grabbed by a ginormous shark and he was trying to tear her in two. "Maybe I ate something…"

Her vision tunneled as she tumbled to the ground.

"Carrie?"

Not Sereana.

She opened her eyes and stared straight into his. "Massimo?"

It couldn't really be him. She was hallucinating, surely. But she felt strong arms close about her. She felt herself lifted and pressed to his broad, hard chest. He was hot and she could hear the thud of his racing heart. Or maybe it was only her own.

If this were just a dream? Fine. She closed her eyes and kept them closed. She would sleep and this awful agony would stop. She really needed it to stop.

"Carrie!"

Don't miss
Revealing Her Nine-Month Secret,
available April 2022 wherever
Harlequin Presents books and ebooks are sold.

Harlequin.com

HPEXP0222

Get 4 FREE REWARDS!

We'll send you 2 FREE Books plus 2 FREE Mystery Gifts.

FREE Value Over **$20**

Both the **Harlequin® Desire** and **Harlequin Presents®** series feature compelling novels filled with passion, sensuality and intriguing scandals.

YES! Please send me 2 FREE novels from the Harlequin Desire or Harlequin Presents series and my 2 FREE gifts (gifts are worth about $10 retail). After receiving them, if I don't wish to receive any more books, I can return the shipping statement marked "cancel." If I don't cancel, I will receive 6 brand-new Harlequin Presents Larger-Print books every month and be billed just $5.80 each in the U.S. or $5.99 each in Canada, a savings of at least 11% off the cover price or 6 Harlequin Desire books every month and be billed just $4.55 each in the U.S. or $5.24 each in Canada, a savings of at least 13% off the cover price. It's quite a bargain! Shipping and handling is just 50¢ per book in the U.S. and $1.25 per book in Canada.* I understand that accepting the 2 free books and gifts places me under no obligation to buy anything. I can always return a shipment and cancel at any time. The free books and gifts are mine to keep no matter what I decide.

Choose one: ☐ **Harlequin Desire**   ☐ **Harlequin Presents Larger-Print**
(225/326 HDN GNND)   (176/376 HDN GNWY)

Name (please print)

Address   Apt. #

City   State/Province   Zip/Postal Code

Email: Please check this box ☐ if you would like to receive newsletters and promotional emails from Harlequin Enterprises ULC and its affiliates. You can unsubscribe anytime.

Mail to the Harlequin Reader Service:
IN U.S.A.: P.O. Box 1341, Buffalo, NY 14240-8531
IN CANADA: P.O. Box 603, Fort Erie, Ontario L2A 5X3

Want to try 2 free books from another series! Call 1-800-873-8635 or visit www.ReaderService.com.

*Terms and prices subject to change without notice. Prices do not include sales taxes, which will be charged (if applicable) based on your state or country of residence. Canadian residents will be charged applicable taxes. Offer not valid in Quebec. This offer is limited to one order per household. Books received may not be as shown. Not valid for current subscribers to the Harlequin Presents or Harlequin Desire series. All orders subject to approval. Credit or debit balances in a customer's account(s) may be offset by any other outstanding balance owed by or to the customer. Please allow 4 to 6 weeks for delivery. Offer available while quantities last.

Your Privacy—Your information is being collected by Harlequin Enterprises ULC, operating as Harlequin Reader Service. For a complete summary of the information we collect, how we use this information and to whom it is disclosed, please visit our privacy notice located at corporate.harlequin.com/privacy-notice. From time to time we may also exchange your personal information with reputable third parties. If you wish to opt out of this sharing of your personal information, please visit readerservice.com/consumerschoice or call 1-800-873-8635. **Notice to California Residents**—Under California law, you have specific rights to control and access your data. For more information on these rights and how to exercise them, visit corporate.harlequin.com/california-privacy.

HDHP22